Pseudepigrapha

Ceci n'est pas un livre.
—*René Magritte*

In this slim volume, on which he spent years of meticulous labor, Tom Newton has created not a mere imitation nor illusory replica but an actual verbatim original work of the 2019 classic *Seven Cries of Delight*.
—*Jorge Luis Borges*

Ironing board, plucked chicken, seven cries, a peach. Eat this book.
—*Salvador Dali*

The book is not the story.
—*Alfred Korzybski*

Seven Cries of Delight
and Other Stories

TOM NEWTON

RECITAL

Seven Cries of Delight

ISBN: 978-1-7337464-0-3
Library of Congress Control Number: 2019942434

RECITAL PUBLISHING
Woodstock, NY 12498
www.recitalpublishing.com

Cover and book design by Bryan Maloney
Author photo by Art Murphy

Many of the stories in this volume have previously appeared online in the podcast The Strange Recital. *The Sound of the Bridge* was first published in the anthology *Skryptor Luminous Volumes*, Aqualamb 2019.

Recital Publishing is an imprint of the online podcast The Strange Recital.
Fiction that questions the nature of reality
www.thestrangerecital.com

Contents

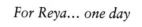

For Reya... one day

The Best of Luck

On a round table the backgammon board is open and abandoned. Three pieces are stacked skew-whiff on the hinged divider and a rose-coloured tumbler lies on its side in one of the trays. The dice are nowhere in evidence. The red and black triangles are still cluttered as if in play, but the players themselves have disappeared. It is not surprising.

I am impressed with Margaret Dillon. She is full of original ideas and the strength to bring them to fruition. She visits occasionally, usually on Fridays. Her creation, in this case, is paradoxical, for the effort and motivation to establish and maintain it, let alone its cost, is in diametrical opposition to what its purpose might be. This is The Idle House. I have been here for almost three months.

The table which supports the backgammon board is on one side of an enclosed courtyard, under a pergola laden with vines. There are two chairs, arranged at unconscious angles. I am looking at them from the opposite wall, seated in a suspended rattan sofa, gently dangling in the late afternoon. A gecko clings to the wall above my head. I have plenty of time to think and have come to see how most of my thoughts are mundane.

If you are a person who dislikes work and has no desire to do anything at all, you can come to The Idle House. You will be sheltered, clothed and fed, free of charge. You can stay here for as long as you want. Admittance is dependent on vacancy, as there are only twelve beds. Guests usually stay until they can no longer stand their own inertia, and then move on, opening up spaces for other lazy people.

1

What is laziness? I know the definition but I am looking for something deeper: the need to describe such a quality in the first place. It seems that there is an abhorrence for anyone who despises work.

It could be linked to the conflict between individual-self interest and group cooperation, or it might have originated with the emergence of agriculture, when a ruling class evolved and people were exhorted to toil. A moral stigma was attached to idleness, further emphasized by religion.

I don't find anything wrong with people providing for others, after all that is what The Idle House does. It is coercion that bothers me. I do not like to be told what to do by anyone, not even myself, for any reason. Perhaps my presence here is due to a residual childhood desire for parental care, never outgrown. Or it could just be fear.

I would like to think I came here on a warm cloud of understanding that had liberated me from the stupidities of life, but I do not. Whatever it is, the word 'Laziness' is much more complex than the dictionary would have you believe, as is 'Love'.

I swing in my chair, these thoughts are mixed with others—the woman in room number seven who never speaks—whether I will scrape the mayonnaise off my sandwich—the number of cicadas I hear at night. I think I am approaching a crisis point where I will feel the need to do something.

In a corner of the courtyard is a pond contained by a curved wall. Water gushes into it from the end of an old pipe, spouting through abundant ivy. There are water-lilies on the surface, and large koi swimming below. It is very beautiful. I have spent a lot of time looking at it and have noticed the magic square that someone has scratched into the cement. Sixteen different numbers laid out in four rows by four rows, each row summing to the number thirty-four no matter which way you make the addition—horizontally, vertically or diagonally.

No one has clearly explained to me the purpose of this establishment. It might be a half-way house for the humane rehabilitation of lazy people into the work force, but that seems far too cynical for Margaret Dillon. I have met her a few times. She is very tall.

There is a small, eclectic library here. When I first arrived I spent a few days looking through it. I haven't read much since then. I discovered some occult esoterica. *The Lesser Key of Solomon* and three grimoires of Agrippa. The sigils of demons caught my attention. They were made by tracing a numerical representation of a name on a magic square.

As the season has grown milder, I've been spending my days in the courtyard and my interest in the grimoires has waned. But now the magic square on the pond wall has brought it back, along with the desire to sigilize my name.

Almost a week has passed since I heard the whisper to action. I have copied the square from the pond on to a piece of card, and I've revisited the library. I made a lipogram from my name by dropping the vowels, and converted the remaining consonants to the numerical value of the respective Hebrew letters. I have drawn my sigil and now I require some maps. As I did this, I realised that I would need a plan, if I were ever to leave. Then I had the idea that I could use the sigil to plot a route. The not completely random arbitrariness of the idea seemed to be a pertinent mode of re-entry into the physical world. My signature would denote my location, not just my name. Geography would become an analog of thought.

There are five numbers in my sigil, two of them are the same. Without even laying it over the map, I can tell that I will be visiting two of the places on the route twice. This itinerary has me start at point A, go to B, and from there to C, then return to the starting point A, and end the journey by going back to C.

This twofold doubling back across the globe intrigues me. It hints at a purpose, both eldritch and obscure, which I am trying to unravel and I haven't even made the journey yet. I am beginning to feel an excitement I have not felt in years. There are atlases in the library. I will start with a projection of the globe and narrow it down from there.

The photocopy machine ejects a map of the world. It is still warm in my hands as I trace the square upon it. Nine, four, five, nine, five—my sigil is a right angled triangle. The starting point, which is the narrow angle, is at the left. I place this point on Miami, the location of The Idle House.

I can understand now the importance once given to naming things, and wish I had been called something else. The first destination, when I leave Miami, is Idar in Gujurat, India. From there I will travel to Tiksi in the Sakha Republic of Russia. A quick search on the library computer tells me that it is not a town but an 'urban-type settlement' sitting on the shores of the Laptev Sea. It has a brutal polar climate and a population of five thousand and sixty-three. It makes me think of Stalin and the Gulag. The trip back to Miami will be a slap in the face and then I will return to the northernmost settlement in Russia. How long I will stay there, I have no idea. I had hoped that my final destination would be a European city but I cannot allow myself to be thwarted by disappointment.

If any of this is to be possible, I will need a grant. The Idle House awards grants in some circumstances. I shall have to write a formal proposal. A request for a paid holiday would be tactless. A voyage of research for educational purposes might work. I could propose a book. Idar has a rich history, stretching back to myth. Tiksi? The book loses its glow.

The act of overlaying a shape on to a map is an artistic idea. This will be my approach. I can elaborate—the triangulation of three places with a personal signature, the melding of the symbolic essence of the individual into the landscape, the condensation of a sublimate etc. etc. Art has the added advantage of a complicated relationship with value, which is hard to define. The application flows easily. When it is finished, I go down from my room, across the courtyard to the office.

The staff at The Idle House have a policy of minimal intrusion, and the office is as empty as usual. I find an envelope in the stationary cupboard, seal up my folded application and drop it into the suggestion/message box which hangs on the wall by the door. I've never put anything of importance in it before. From time to time I deposit a note suggesting a suggestion box. I never tire of the looping absurdity and wonder about its effect.

"Oh God. Not another note about a suggestion box."

As soon as the paper has left my hand, a sense of waiting develops. It is a subconscious rumbling. The ogre has stirred and wants to go outside. I am still excited but the initial joy has dispersed.

Weeks go by. Every day I check the mailbox for room number five, sometimes more than once. A fumbling with the little key and a quick glance inside. Nothing but air. Then at last there is an envelope. I tear it open where I stand.

... thank you for your interesting proposal. We have given it careful consideration and regret to inform you that your application has been denied.

We wish you the best of luck ...

❖

The Best of Luck was inspired by Marcel Duchamp's idea of *'Une maison des paresseux'*.

Mr Moreno's Shoes

Luis Moreno ate his own shoes—both of them. It wasn't as if he was adrift on an ocean, alone in an uncovered boat, driven half mad from drinking brine and from the radiation of the sun beating down relentlessly upon him, with no food but his shoes—in other words a desperate act for survival. It wasn't that, although he might have felt it was.

Mr Moreno lived downtown. He was an office worker of scant importance to his employer, meaning that he could easily be replaced. This is exactly what happened the day he arrived at work in his socks. He offered no explanation. It was a silence almost as perverse as the contents of his strange meal. But nothing was known about that, and he quietly left just as he had arrived—shoeless. It was raining.

Moreno had determination, cutting strips of shoe leather and boiling them until they were chewable, grating the heels and eating them by the spoonful. The soles had been a challenge. It had taken six weeks.

"Nothing comes from nowhere" his father used to say. It was one of those many platitudes to which he was prone. To Luis as a boy they had always seemed to hold some undefined wisdom. From the vantage point of adulthood, he had come to think that these banalities were an unconscious attempt to grasp at meaning.

His father had spent his life working as a cobbler, as had his grandfather before him. Not so Luis. On account of his mother's machinations with the church, he had been enrolled as a medical student in Madrid but he never became a doctor. He dropped out soon after starting. By the time he was twenty-five he was looking for a way to leave Spain. His short time as a student was spent associating with poets, painters and philosophers. It was a brief experience with lasting consequences.

Nothing came from nowhere, so everything must have come from somewhere. Over breakfast one morning in Madrid, he had set fire to his hair with a cigarette lighter. Already in his youth he displayed a penchant for impulsive acts but none of them were what they seemed. He had planned the hair burning for months, waiting for the quiff that swung across his forehead to grow long enough to be worth setting ablaze. Even the day had been carefully chosen, taking into consideration the people who would be present and their likely states of mind. It was a gathering of friends, all of them hungover from the previous night, including Luis. He suddenly roused them from their torpor by flicking his lighter and burning off his quiff—a part of his anatomy of which he was quite proud. It disappeared within seconds and never grew back the same way. His friends were all delightfully shocked. Luis had a wicked sense of humour. He was obviously one of those people—those surrealists.

They laughed again when Luis collapsed on the street outside the café, and rolled around cupping his hands together. They laughed until they realized he was having a seizure. He had three such incidents over the next few months and then nothing thereafter, although he never knew what to expect and always avoided looking directly at shining objects or reflections. Each time he lost consciousness he woke to find himself walking in a densely forested landscape. He would wander for hours, never seeing another living creature, until he came to a few seconds later.

Luis Moreno left Spain in 1935, not long before the outbreak of the civil war. The rest of his family stayed behind, aligning themselves with the Republicans. He went first to Paris, then to London and finally to New York where he stayed. There were a number of expatriate Spanish artists living in Paris at the time and soon he had crossed paths with most of them.

Through them he had a brush with surrealism but he was disappointed. Though left-leaning himself, he didn't like the way their pettifogging and political bickering had ruptured the movement he admired. The surrealists he met didn't think much of the shy Spaniard beyond his occasional, interesting outbursts of extreme extroversion. He didn't do anything. He didn't write, or paint, or make films. He planned extensively of course, but that wasn't apparent to them and even if it had been, they probably would not have approved.

He had a tenacity that reminded him of vindictiveness, the same doggedness as someone who waits years to avenge a slight. But there the similarity ceased. There was nothing particularly malicious about him. He just liked to make plans. That meant he spent a lot of time daydreaming in exquisite detail. It was a conceptual art, not for the purpose of his own gain, though not excluding it either. He understood that movements in art, like fashion, were defined by their times. Surrealism would have its day, and when that day was over, its capacity to shock would dwindle into the mainstream. Even British monarchs would one day have surrealist paintings in their royal collection. The movement would become history and its value would increase. To that end, he bought paintings from unknown artists with promise whenever he could. In New York he bought several from the young, yet-to-be famous Jackson Pollock. Luis wasn't constrained by time because he moved with it. He knew he would have a source of income in the future.

When he first arrived in New York, he made money by giving Spanish lessons. His students were mostly from the affluent classes and most of them were women. He had been helped by his friend René Duval, a French art dealer with connections in New York. René made it his business to know wealthy people. They had met in Paris, and it was on René's urging that he had decided to come to America. He helped Luis find a small apartment on 14th Street, lent him some money to get him started, and suggested he give lessons to support himself. He even found him his first clients. Despite his arduous social climbing, René was generous and without him Luis would have had much more difficulty establishing himself. By this time he was almost fluent in English, albeit with a thick accent, which charmed his female students. He had a knack for languages.

René later became very successful and it was to him Luis turned when it came time to sell his paintings. But that was much later. They remained lifelong friends. René was one of the few people who was able to recognize the kind of artist he was. Luis even spoke to him about his shoe-eating idea, which René considered vaguely Oedipal, though he didn't disapprove.

The idea had first come to him when he saw the shoe-shine men at Grand Central station. Among the throngs of passengers, he came across rough-hewn thrones in which men reclined and had their shoes polished by other men who squatted, or sat on small stools at their feet. It wasn't the obvious social implication that caught his eye but the proximity of head to feet. These were usually extremities, as far apart on a body as anything could be. In this case they were not. It didn't matter that there were more bodies than one. The idea was the same, or at least had the same effect on him. It came to him unformulated, as an inchoate mist that hung in his brain. In his usual fashion he gradually sculpted it, constantly adapting it as situations changed, carefully filling in details as if colouring a drawing, until it led years later to the day when he ate his shoes and sold his paintings.

One of his first students was Sabrina Gibbs. She was the youngest of two daughters from a wealthy and cloyingly controlling family. She soon found herself in a romantic relationship with Luis. She had artistic aspirations and a natural talent as a painter, and no need to work. In fact she was not expected to work, just to get married to a suitable bachelor. She found these expectations to be a crushing burden, so contrary to her nature. Her parents tolerated her Spanish lessons with some suspicion. Perhaps it was an act of rebellion that attracted her to Luis, along with his dark and lavish good looks, or it might have been his bohemian lifestyle that drew her to him. When she first came to his apartment, she was impressed by its utilitarian sparseness. He had barely no more than a bed to sleep in, with paintings leaning haphazardly against the walls. He only had one suit of clothes that he cleaned meticulously with a damp cloth. He seemed to be completely unconcerned with all the things that her parents obsessed about. It was exciting and liberating. Such a life was possible.

When she announced a few months later that they were engaged to be married there was a volcanic eruption within the family. The Spanish lessons were immediately discontinued. The pleasant but oily René Duval, who had introduced them, was no longer welcome in the house. She was threatened with disinheritance. A European trip would have been in order, had it not been for the worsening situation on that continent.

Before her parents could do anything rash, Sabrina and Luis were secretly married at City Hall. They picked up some cheap rings on the way there, which she paid for. Afterwards they had a small party with a group of friends at the apartment on 14th Street. René had filled the bathtub with ice and bottles of champagne. It was a good start to a new life.

Unfortunately, it quickly became apparent to her that the marriage was not going to work. She began to see a side of Luis that she had been unaware of before—he seemed completely unmotivated, lying for hours each day on his bed staring up at the ceiling and not responding when she spoke to him. At first she let him be and went about her painting but as the months passed it bothered her more and more. He was cold and remote, obviously so used to living alone that he was unable to share his life with anyone. Selfish really. The thought of spending years like this, going nowhere, became unbearable to her. Of course she didn't understand that when he was lying motionless on the bed he was involved in acts just as creative as she was when painting. He never told her. He also never spoke to her of his thoughts about the relationship between truth and belief. He was of the opinion that no one saw ghosts unless they believed in them. Or inversely, if you saw a dog crossing the road in front of you, you saw it because you believed in the existence of dogs. In other words, reality was partly a judgement based on its perception. He was aware of her growing disappointment in him and recognized the truth of what she thought in relation to her belief but he did nothing and let it play out, as he felt that all people were entitled to their beliefs.

The final straw was when he took a second-rate job, as far as she was concerned, in the mailroom at the Steinway piano factory in Astoria. She tried to talk him out of it but he was adamant. She packed her bags and left.

That first night without her he dreamed of three rectangles, nested inside each other and viewed from above against a field of blackness. He felt it should be important but could never make any sense of it.

As much as he was depressed about the collapse of his marriage, Sabrina's parents were overjoyed. They helped her get a divorce and her inheritance was restored. They wrote the whole thing off as youthful folly from a girl who was too headstrong for her own good. Luckily there were no children.

Contrary to Sabrina's beliefs, Luis was perfectly capable of applying himself. He had come to the conclusion that a second-rate job was exactly what he needed. Once the decision was made, he acted on it promptly. He wanted a job that paid enough for his modest needs but not enough for the temptation of wealth to distract him. It had to have minimal prospects of advancement, limited responsibility, and be easy to do. It should be far enough away from where he lived to reduce the possibility of social interactions with his co-workers. He wanted to fulfil his duties without forming emotional attachments. He wanted a job he could easily walk away from—in his socks. The mailroom at Steinway & Sons fitted those criteria. Aside from any unforeseen events, he planned to eat his shoes in about twenty years. After that he would wait until Franco died, and return to Spain.

Those occasional extreme outbursts that had intrigued the surrealists in Paris were not as unconscious as they had imagined. He used them as a means to release the tension caused by holding innumerable details in his mind over long periods of time. While he was in New York he refrained from such activity as he did not want to jeopardize his immigrant status.

So he went to work in his boring job and stayed there for many years. He was always punctual, responsible, efficient and personable. He was liked well enough but not well liked, as no one was ever able to get to know him and could never understand why. He remained a mystery who was not thought about too much—just as he wanted. He used his first pay check to buy a pair of Italian shoes. He had done some research and found that these would be the most suitable to eat as the leather was relatively thin and he liked their style.

On the fateful day he got up, threw away his remaining shoes, the ones he hadn't eaten— just two pairs, chewed the last strip of leather he had been saving for that day, followed by a slice of toast, and then went to work.

When it was noticed that he wasn't wearing any shoes, there was great surprise and consternation in the mailroom. It was so unexpected and out of character. He didn't bat an eyelid and carried on as usual as his colleagues gave him sidelong glances and muttered among themselves. Finally he was summoned to his supervisor's office. Mr Clifford came around to the front of his desk as he entered.

"What happened to your shoes, Moreno?"

Luis felt a huge sense of relief well up inside him. He was beginning to enjoy himself. He had nothing to lose. He didn't reply, just shrugged and stared down at his feet. There was a small hole in his right sock through which his big toe was slightly visible.

"Are you alright? Do you need medical attention?"

"No thank you. I am very well. How are you?"

"You can't work here without proper attire. You should know that."

"Yes sir."

Mr Clifford was perplexed. Luis could sense him searching for the way out of an inexplicable situation.

"You've been with us for years. What's going on?"

Luis shrugged again, in a particularly Spanish way. He could see that Clifford had made up his mind.

"I see. Well, I don't know what's come over you but you are relieved of your duties as of now. Go home. Get some help."

Luis slipped out of the factory. He walked the streets in the rain and took the subway, all the time enjoying the embarrassed attention he received. People looked, then looked away, then looked again, and then turned away as he met their eye. It couldn't be better. The perfect culmination to twenty years of work. He was euphoric.

As he made his way to René's apartment on 57th Street to discuss the sale of the paintings, which was already pending, his whole body tingled with satisfaction. The weight of the last twenty, even thirty years had been lifted from him and he felt as if he might float away. The idea had come to him in New York, though he had been reaching for it ever since he left medical school. Now his work was done and he had earned his freedom. These days artists seemed to think that they had to keep cranking out work, probably because of the way the art world had evolved into the economy. To him they were missing the point and the depth of their creations diminished accordingly. He had always believed that an artwork should take a lifetime to produce. Quantity was not in the same league as quality.

The doorman at René's building did not seem to be at all concerned with his lack of footwear. Luis climbed the four flights of stairs and rang the bell. The door opened revealing René in a silk smoking jacket, a cigar clenched in his jaw. He looked down.

"I see you've finally eaten your shoes. Congratulations. We should celebrate."

Intervals

I've chosen to see the relationships between people as intervals. It's a musical metaphor but not out of place. We are all vibrations of a sort, just not all at the same frequency. I can picture numerous sine waves, peaks and troughs, making a tangled diagram. It's all about frequency and amplitude. That's all it is.

There's a thrill to following a metaphor when it veers from poetry toward pedantry, splitting hairs and brushing them aside, yearning for fulfilment.

I could dispense with the musical connection and imagine intervals purely as gaps—undefined amounts of empty space, but then I would be denying myself the pleasure of examining my relationships in terms of Thirds, Fifths, Ninths, Sevenths and Perfect Fourths, as well as the additional bonus of augmentation or suspension.

As much as the original vibrations are a matter of frequency and amplitude, their interpretation, or arrangement as intervals is about harmony and dissonance. The metaphor smirks at me with smug self-congratulation, because relationships are concerned with the same things.

≀

I start with something simple. Saturday mornings, sitting in front of the television with my friend Eddy Michaels. We are banging on surfaces in a kind of frenetic joy with anything that comes to hand as we watch cartoons and wait for his mother to bring us food. Ravioli from a can. Delicious. I save his life by grabbing his wrist and preventing him from sliding off the gently pitched garage roof. We are best friends. We play on the stairs in

15

his house. Once something disappears completely. There, then gone—just like that. We are both amazed but easily accept the mystery for what it is. What interval would describe us?

An Octave seems the best. Though the notes are separated by more semitones than some of the other intervals, their frequency ratio is simple—2:1, just a doubling. Unison.

This idea has no merit. No truth at all. No depth. But I'm learning from it. The differences between people are not caused by distance. They are harmonic—the sound of different distances you might say.

It is a summer evening and I am walking down Ninth Avenue on the West side of the street. It has been a hot and humid day but the temperature is becoming more pleasant. I am wearing my usual shorts and wife-beater. I don't beat my wife. I'm not even married. It's a misnomer.

The avenue is full of cars, almost at a standstill, horns blaring impatiently though there is nowhere to go. It is urban frustration. The flip side of opportunity. The air is full of fumes.

I am happy, gliding through the throngs of people, side-stepping the slow ones and those who stop suddenly for no reason. Most likely tourists. The light is fading. A tall man crosses in front of me as a yellow taxi pulls over and the rear door begins to open. A man steps out. The tall man has a gun in his hand, aimed at the emerging passenger. In his other hand he holds up a police badge. The passenger stops mid-exit. I have never seen such a look of surprise on anyone's face before or since. I feel I'm the only one who has noticed. It's a private moment but I keep on walking. My destination is the Turkish restaurant around the corner. This is where my girlfriend has arranged to meet me. She likes Turkish food. We eat olives for breakfast.

I think we are separated by a Minor Seventh, if only because in harmonic theory this interval is often regarded as needing resolution and we don't have that. Not at all. Perhaps this is why she never meets me at the restaurant as arranged, and I eat alone—shepherd's salad, hummus, bread.

Napoleon said that metaphysicians should be thrown into ponds. I'm not quite sure why. His words strike a dissonant chord, and not just because of their protofascist ring. They make me aware of how my own compulsive metaphysics annoy me. Surely there are better things to do. My constant speculation is not an attempt to answer life's questions. I threw truth and meaning from a window long ago. They lie shattered on the pavement, kicked aside or stepped on by pedestrians, and noticed only by children who gather them up for their games.

The attempt to view personal relationships as intervals is also a game—with pieces that have no particular shape. There's nothing wrong with that. It is the compulsion that is problematic. It chips away at the edifice of free will.

There is also a degree of mapping involved—take one concept and overlay it on another. Take the result and overlay that on to something else. Repeat, repeat, repeat. It seems a natural function, or capability of the brain, and as far as we know the brain is situated in the left hand.

Here I go again. I can't stop.

Perhaps what Napoleon meant was that sudden immersion in cold water would shock the metaphysicians from their babble. I will take a cold shower when I get home and see if he was right.

That mapping of concepts upon each other irritates some people.

"Suppose you are not you, and that you are in fact a stray dog..."

"But I am me. I'm not a dog."

"I know, I know. But just assume for a minute that this is how things are."

"Why would I do that? Things are not this way."

My palm goes to my forehead. There's no point. I lapse into silence.

It doesn't take me long to finish my food but it is dark when I leave the restaurant. The streets are just as busy. I look around and wonder what interval would express my relationship to people I don't know. Could I assume that the veil of ignorance would be an homogenizing influence and render the same result for every stranger? Knowing not to assume anything, I imagine the same interval would suffice for all.

It would have to be a Perfect Fourth. I like the sound of the name. That's one good reason. The connection of that particular adjective with the unknown is deeply pleasing. The number four suggests a square. That combination of straight lines is surprising. I would expect the unknown to be murky with unclear borders and better suited to curves. But the square is one facet of a cube, which is the form of a die. Dice are tools that allow chance to manifest as numbers. So with a little tortuous reasoning I can make the number Four represent chance viewed in two dimensions.

None of this has anything to do with the musical metaphor and I search my limited knowledge of Harmony to find justification for my instincts.

There's a film crew working ahead of me and a production assistant prevents me from going where I want. Two actors are leaving a bar and appear to be having an argument. I can't make out what they are saying from where I'm standing. They do it again and again. It is meant to be winter and they are bundled in overcoats, hats and scarves. Chipped ice lies on the ground around them and fake snow falls from above. I watch for a while with dull fascination as they spin the dreams of culture, and then I turn away to find a different route.

⟨

The Perfect Fourth was used quite frequently in the Middle Ages, when Western music theory was in its infancy. The fact that this interval is perfect means that it is neither minor nor major, which metaphorically fits with relationships to strangers. In medieval music the Perfect Fourth ran parallel to the melodic line. That suggests to me unknown lives running concurrently but separately, though maybe I am trying too hard to make things fit.

As time passed and perceptions changed, the interval which had generally been regarded as a consonance came, at least under certain circumstances to be viewed as dissonant. In twentieth century atonal music it didn't matter anymore.

If there is such a thing as a right track, I am on it. The Perfect Fourth, neither minor nor major with both dissonance and consonance, is the perfect interval to describe my relationship to people I don't know.

It is much harder getting home than I expected. I bypass the obstacle of the film shoot and turn on to 45th Street. Almost immediately my way is blocked by a police cordon. Apparently a crane has fallen—one of those giant claws that aids and abets the construction of the towers. The multi-faceted structures of glass and steel reach up into the sky. They are systematically replacing the buildings of the old town and the livelihoods they contain. No doubt the old town had replaced an older one, I just hadn't been alive to witness it. In my mind I place onion domes on the top of each one, until a coldly modern Kremlin looms above me.

Most of midtown on the west side has been closed off, so it is impossible for me to reach the subway at Times Square. I'll find a different way but it's getting late and service is interrupted at night due to the dilapidated state of the infrastructure.

As I walk east on 46th Street I wonder what caused the crane to fall. Cost cutting? Corruption? Shoddy operation? These days when anything happens, the first thought for most people is terrorism, so propagandised have we all become. But to me it seems more like the punishment of luxury. That covers it.

I'm beginning to create another scenario.

That object, lost so long ago at the bottom of Eddy Michaels' stairs—what was it? A toy? A box?

I remember now. It was a little glass tube with a sealed metal cap. It was filled with a transparent liquid. We had no idea what it was but it looked strange and dangerous. We didn't have much time to learn more because it vanished soon after we had found it.

Now I know where it is. Things that disappear can reappear just as easily. All I have to do is look in the gutter. I move to the curb and peer over. Using the light from my phone I look more closely and there it is, peeking out from beneath a crushed paper cup. I gently scuff the cup away with my foot and squat down. The cap has gone. The tube is empty. I stay hunkered down for a while, then without touching it I stand up again.

There goes civilization.

World Leader Retired

I knew him when we were young. We were friends for a few months. Then we lost touch. He had a remarkable sense of direction—innate and much more powerful than most people's. It was as if he carried in his mind a very detailed map of everywhere, and he was able to consult it at any time, with no apparent effort. This meant that if he knew where he wanted to go, he could always get there. It is the only thing I remember about him. That and the fact that he could be annoying, as he often needed somewhere to stay and would show up at any time unannounced.

But he paid for the hospitality he received by facilitating travel. We would be driving at night through unfamiliar streets. From the passenger seat he would calmly announce which turn to take. He was never wrong, even though he had never been to where we were going. This was an era before the advent of GPS, the Internet and mobile phones.

Now of course he is old like me, and retired. Except—unlike me, he is famous. I had forgotten about him for close to fifty years when he suddenly reappeared as a candidate for political office, and not just any office, but the presidency itself. And he won. That was some years ago. Now he is a world leader retired.

I didn't spend much time thinking about it beyond an occasional dalliance in delayed incredulity. How could he have come from nowhere to that position? It would be as if I found myself running the army one day. It could just be that I haven't been paying attention and that there is a lot I don't know.

He would not have been haunting my memories, except

that I just saw him on the street and everything came back. I wondered if he was searching for somewhere to stay and hoped it was not my place he was looking for. I could imagine him ringing the doorbell while I was eating dinner.

I saw him outside OK CUTZ, which as the name implies is a low-end barbershop. I don't know if he had been there for a haircut or just happened to be passing by. As I don't work anymore and survive on a lacklustre pension, OK CUTZ seemed a good enough place for me to get groomed. I was becoming intrigued and hoped I might glean some information by going in there.

I decided to get a number one buzz cut. I think an old man with severely short hair is someone to be reckoned with. Once I overheard two young men talking. They were saying that old men always get short haircuts because they are trying to hide their baldness by embracing it. They were laughing. I'm not bald, and if I was I wouldn't care. I'm way beyond such concerns.

I took a seat against the wall to wait my turn and picked up a faded magazine from the glass table. A girl was sweeping up hair from the floor. Her expression was an acceptance of the mild frustration and boredom that came with the job. I looked beyond her around the room, half hoping to see some evidence of a presidential visit. There was none.

The magazine was quite old and the affairs it contained had long since been current but I found an interesting article about the invention of LSD and its use in psychiatry. I read of Albert Hoffman and of a woman who gave birth to the world, of a man who became everything, and of faces whose eyes dripped with worms and maggots. The article was doubly interesting, not only in its subject matter but also in the way that it was portrayed as contemporary. It made me think about time, and that flicked a mental switch.

I never had time to finish it, as the girl who had been sweeping the floor was beckoning to me. She wanted me to accompany her deeper into the room to an old chair that backed up on to a sink with a cutaway for the neck. It suggested an executioner's block. She intended to wash my hair. I hadn't bargained for that. No one had asked me if I wanted my hair washed and I suspected it was a ploy to extract more money. But I followed her anyway without complaint.

I lay back and put my neck in the slot. A certain degree of trust was required for that. She turned on the tap and gently wet my hair with both hands. Then she massaged my scalp with shampoo, working quickly, leaning close over me. Her breasts brushed my shoulder. I could smell her perfume. I closed my eyes. There was an intimacy to the whole experience. A solitary intimacy. I wondered if she felt it too. I couldn't know. She never said a word. But somehow I suspected not. It was different for her. She had to physically deal with strangers each day, massaging their heads and sweeping up their dead hair, witnessing their imperfections from close up. It was most likely a chore, forgotten as soon as possible. She gave me a towel to dry my own hair and motioned me towards the barber chair.

I am generally not one for small-talk. Like flattery it does not trip easily from my tongue. But today I was going to have to make a special effort. The barber awaited me with a smile. Once I had climbed into the chair he quickly tucked a cloth around my neck and whipped a cover over me. My hands disappeared on my lap. He swung the chair towards the mirror.

"What's it going to be, boss?"

"Number one buzz cut."

"Number one too short. Number three better."

"If you say so."

"Number one—you bald guy. You don't want bald guy."

"Okay."

The barber had a shock of dark and greasy hair and a close-cut pointed beard of the same colour, which gave him a Mephistophelean look. He pulled a buzz clipper from the counter and went around behind me.

I couldn't place his accent. I assumed he was South American.

"Where are you from?"

"Belarus. You?"

"I'm English."

"My brother live in London. When we come from our country we go first in London. Then I come here."

"Did you cut hair in your country?"

"No. I work for KGB."

This was interesting. Then I saw him grinning at me in the mirror. He was joking. A wry one. He'd convinced me. How could I know all that had happened in those Cold War years? There was a man killed with a poisoned umbrella. That I remember. Strange times. I can almost feel nostalgic for them now. But that's a stupid way to think. As if the suffering of the past is any less than that of the present. Suffering can't be differentiated. It is like water—filling up any available space.

"You ever cut hair for famous people?"

"Sure boss. Every day." He grinned again.

"Has a president ever been in?"

"The President? Why he come here? Unless he look for my niece."

We both looked down the room for the girl with the broom but she wasn't there.

After that I lost interest in the conversation, shut my eyes and let him finish the job. When I left I glanced at my reflection in the window to see how the haircut looked. Not bad. Though in hindsight I should have trusted myself and gone with the number one.

So the ex-president hadn't been for a haircut when I saw him. I could rule that out. That left the question as to what he was doing in the area and why I hadn't noticed anyone else recognizing him. I hadn't seen any Secret Service people either. If it had been any other childhood friend I came across, who I hadn't seen for years, I might have doubted myself. But because he had been president I knew exactly what he looked like, I'd seen so many photographs. There could be no doubt—it was Neil Godfrey. Something was just not right about it.

I couldn't put it down. As I walked home through the park, I felt like a kitten batting at a ball of yarn, catching my claws in it, causing it to unravel and tangle. Unable to stop, yet with no comprehension. Does a cat understand a ball of yarn? Not its human purpose. There must be planes of comprehension among all species. I found the complexity almost overwhelming.

There was a lot of squirrel activity as I walked through the park, and I stopped to watch them for a while. They raced up and down trees with their jerky, shimmering motions, seemingly intent on gathering acorns. It was that time of year. Squirrels and other animals share the city with people. Our existences overlap but mostly we are separate. We occupy the same geographical space but, as with comprehension, we live on completely different planes.

It is all a matter of time, which itself is only a measurement, or really a number of measurements. There is the crude division into three—past, present and future. I could see the past as memory, the future as possibility and the present as the interstitial point between them. The present might be measured in those ambiguous units of moments. But how long is a moment? Three seconds? More? Less? Could the future be measured as a negative number of moments?

Alongside this, there is a type of calibration to different clocks—like those of genetics, light and darkness, planetary movement, cellular ageing, and radioactive half-life. Maybe you could do away with measurement entirely and see it as a flowing continuum, in which case the present probably does not exist, being just a way of watching the past become the future. As arbitrary as the way that years are organized into decades.

I had the growing feeling that Neil's unexplained appearance had something to do with this idea of time and different temporal planes. It might also justify his uncanny sense of direction, his mysterious ascent to high office and his equally mysterious disappearance from consciousness. How it could do that, I didn't know. It was intuition.

When I got home I went straight to the fridge. I was hungry. I lived alone in a small place. It was a simple life. I tried to imbue every aspect of it with beauty, and that included the food

I ate. Beauty offered the prospect of happiness. I set the green bowl on the table. Lentil salad with finely chopped parsley, garlic, olives, cucumbers, avocados and feta cheese. It had been marinating in lemon juice while the KGB agent was cutting my hair. I poured myself a glass of red wine and broke off a piece of baguette with my hands. I raised the fork to my mouth and was just experiencing the tangy first taste of lemon when the buzzer interrupted me. I got up and pressed the 'talk' button on the intercom.

"Who is it?"

"I know it's been years, but could I sleep on your couch tonight? I'm sorry. I'll explain..."

Project 4A

"What if I call you Veron?"

"It's not exactly flattering."

"You're from another world, man. Way beyond the solar system. Out there in the psychoverse."

"It has an Ancient Greek sound to it—like Solon. Either that or Star Trek."

Veronica looked up at her companion. His thick, dark hair bounced on his shoulders. He was solid and robust, which was probably why Rose had cast him as the navvy. The pneumatic drill might be a problem. How was the audience going to hear what was going on? It was so loud. But Rose had insisted on it.

"Who's Solon?"

"He was an Athenian statesman and sage. A reformer and a poet."

"A wise politician?"

"I guess so."

"Far out."

On the corner of Prince and Mercer Streets, a car was raised on concrete blocks, all four wheels missing, windows smashed. A gnome-like figure suddenly sprang out from behind it. Veronica recoiled in a spasm of fear but Daniel barely seemed to notice. The gnome ambled off down Prince Street, a grimy plastic bag swinging at his side.

How differently they experienced life. He was so viscerally unaware of the fear a woman felt. Women had to be on their guard. He could just plough through without noticing. But with the fear came a certain sensibility, a capacity for deeper appreciation than brawn alone could provide. She knew that the city bristled

27

with dangers through which she must find her way. In return it bestowed a crazy energy that made everything more vivid.

Veronica. She had never quite felt that she belonged to her name, or it to her. Perhaps a name mysteriously charted the course of a person's life, or alternatively that course defined the name. The Egyptians had recognized the importance of names. Maybe her own had led her to become an actress, like that other Veronica—Miss Lake. That was a pseudonym and probably explained the alcoholism and slew of broken marriages. Beyond their names and vocations they shared a shock of long blond hair that had the tendency to fall over one eye and had the power to unlock many doors. But Veronica Lake was trapped in the 1940s, whereas she had the modern freedom of Now—the time to turn all of that old repression on its head and inside out.

Daniel was absorbed in his own thoughts as they walked down Mercer Street towards the studio. The main thing that clawed at him was the fear that he would be sent to Vietnam. His number was twenty-five. That was bad. It was just a matter of time. He was going to have to do something. But what? He could go to Canada like many of his friends. Maybe he could be a conscientious objector or take an overdose before the physical. The machine was out to get him but they'd have to find him first. He had never registered with the draft and had moved around a lot. But still... the pressure never let up. One thing he knew—he wasn't going to take part in any war for this wretched kakistocracy. He had just discovered that word, and was quite pleased with himself—a form of government in which the worst persons were in power. Veron would be proud of him. She seemed so wise and beautiful. She could run rings around him without even trying.

All of a sudden she broke into a sprint and tore off, coming to an abrupt stop at the curb on Broome Street a block away, and stood there looking at the sky. It took him by surprise and he hurried to join her. She cut a lithe figure in her black leotards and T-shirt, which she always wore to rehearsals.

"What's up? You okay?" He was slightly out of breath.

"I'm fine."

"Why did you take off like that?"

"I was waking myself up. We are all half-asleep, living in a dream. It distracts us from ourselves. When the chatter in my head gets too loud I take action."

"What if you are just dreaming that you are waking from a dream?"

One of these days she would have to tell him about Gurdjieff's teachings. Or maybe not. She liked Daniel well enough but he was over keen on her in a way she did not reciprocate. He was a kid. Their age difference of five years was significant. It was becoming a burden, and she wanted to be light.

The studio was halfway down the block between Broome and Grand. The window was papered over from the inside. There was a sign in it which said 'The Improbable Theater Ensemble', and below that: 'Project 4A, Tonight 7:30pm'.

It was a loft building. The theatre company had the ground floor. Rose, the director lived on the floor above with her husband Fabian, who was also the production designer. The remaining floors were occupied by artists and drug dealers. There were rehearsals every day between ten and six, and performances at night when the company was in New York. The whole building vibrated with a frenzied hum of experimentation and artistic creation. Veronica saw it as the avant-garde of the avant-garde, a beacon, or a great ship cutting through dark waters, blazing with light.

Daniel found a battered hub-cap outside the door and brought it in with him, tossing it on to the huge pile of garbage behind the stages. Everyone called it 'The Mountain'. It was Fabian's idea—an ever growing heap of detritus comprised of old appliances, scraps of plastic, shoes, newspapers, books, stereo equipment, discarded motors, a lawn-mower, bicycles, car tires and even some scrap military hardware—anything they could find to create the physical representation and embodiment of the consumer society.

Rose glowered at them through her glasses. The rest of the cast was already there.

"You're late."

Veronica could tell that Rose was in one of her moods.

"Let's get to work."

Rose was petite and compact. Her small body contradicted the huge spirit it contained, both benign and monstrous. She had a sharp, roving intelligence and an encyclopedic knowledge. Memory like a steel trap—as they often joked. All these qualities were offset by a burning, volcanic furnace which could erupt at any time with shocking intensity. Though her rages seemed to come suddenly from nowhere, there were in fact signs of an onset which Veronica had learned to recognize after three years with the company—a steely tensing of the cheeks, and eyes that looked without seeing. She recognized them now.

The production they were about to rehearse and perform later that night was a piece called 'Project 4A'. It consisted of three plays acted simultaneously on three different stages. It had sprung from Rose's mind as a spark that kindled the actors, who then created it through improvisation. Rose would criticize and direct their efforts. There was no script in the traditional sense, but over the course of a year the improvisations had gelled into a script of sorts that could be abandoned and returned to at will. The seven actors were so finely attuned to each other and so familiar with the piece, that changes came easily to them, as smooth as knives through butter.

There were three circular stages arranged in a gentle crescent. The 'mountain' rose from behind the space between the left and centre stages. There was minimal use of scenery. Fabian, who was quite brilliant, had built a giant ear (about six feet tall) that automatically swung towards the source of a sound. He would wheel it out between the stages whenever he felt like it. Fabian also handled the lighting with his usual expertise. There was a large screen at the back of the room that he usually washed with slowly changing colours. He also painted images on glass and projected them. Occasionally, when he had taken acid, things could get more extreme and unexpected. It just added to the chaos that was always present in their performances.

Veronica worked mostly on the centre stage, where she played Bridget O'Shaughnessy in a rendition of *The Maltese Falcon*. It was the ensemble's interpretation of the story and was not a faithful copy of the original. Sam Spade was played by Raoul Caldon, whose chiseled face worked well for the part. He had kept his hair short during the course of the production to allow the fedora to rest convincingly on his head. He would don a wig when he played different parts. All the actors had multiple roles in Project 4A.

On the left stage was a drama that Rose had created from Hindu myth. It was the most difficult and mysterious of the three plays. She had instructed the actors to dispense with time. For actors, timing was almost everything, and they struggled to understand her intentions.

"Myths are stories that are recreated every day," she said. "Only time makes us see them as ancient. Without it there would be no differentiation between science fiction and history. So, get rid of it."

Most cultures have tales of a sacrificed god—of how his body was dismembered and the parts scattered, of how the body could never be completely reassembled. The meaning of these stories is not static. It is ever shifting and seeps into a person like poetry. Myth was the meeting point of mind and nature. "But you would be foolish to separate those things." That's what Rose thought.

They came to call this play 'The Sacrifice'. It was so lacking in plot and motivation that Veronica had found it a challenge at first, as they all did. Eventually she was able to relax into it and found its dreamlike quality liberating. It increased her awareness like psychotherapy might. Rose was furiously insistent that they avoid any kind of allegorical representation.

"You are not wooden copies of yourselves. You are flames twisting in a fire. You are writhing snakes."

Project 4A opened with The Sacrifice. The lights would fade to darkness, which Fabian let linger until he felt the audience become restless. At the moment when their expectation began turning to boredom, the screen would begin to glow. Then the audience would see the coupling of the Progenitor Prajāpati with his daughter Uṣás, the goddess of dawn, as giant silhouettes of antelopes. Fabian used shadow puppets to create the effect. The scene was accompanied by the sound of birds, emanating from a reel-to-reel, which he operated from the lighting booth. Suddenly an arrow—in reality a bamboo skewer pulled to its target with a thread, pierced Prajāpati. The lights faded up on the left stage, revealing an archer lowering his bow. The other stages remained in darkness.

The archer was played by Daniel. For most of the production he worked on the right stage, building a house. This sub-play was known as 'Material', and was primarily a one-man act. He would frame out a building—sawing and hammering through the course of the evening. He could not finish it in one night, and so in each performance he would continue from where he had left off the night before, until it was complete. Then it would be torn down and he would start again from scratch. There was a Sisyphean quality to it. Occasionally he would chip away at concrete blocks with a pneumatic drill. This was one of Rose's recent ideas. She liked to tweak the production constantly. It would produce an ear-splitting noise, drowning out any dialogue from the other stages. Rose was very pleased with it. She said that Daniel was her big, little navvy.

Veronica wondered about that word, and looked it up later. A navvy was an unskilled labourer. It might be a shortened form of 'navigator'. What was so unskilled about navigating? Unless the word had a different meaning at an earlier time, or Rose was subconsciously implying that Daniel had to navigate his way through plays he did not understand. But then who did?

"Right then, let's take it from the section where Sam comes to visit Miss O'Shaughnessy at her apartment." Rose had sat down in a chair in the front row. Fabian raised the lights on the centre stage, leaving the other two stages in darkness.

"Where's Cordy?"

"I think she went to the bathroom."

"Ugh!" Rose winced as Cordelia reappeared, unaware of her error.

"Cordy, get up there on the middle stage with Bridget O'Shaughnessy. You can be her atman for this scene."

The atman, in Hinduism, was the essence of life, or the self. Through enlightenment it would merge with Brahman. It was originally Veronica's idea for an actor to have an atman. This would be represented by another actor who would be present in a scene, but unnoticed and non-reactive, merely observing in silence. Rose had liked the idea and taken it as her own.

They'd had long discussions about it. Could a woman have an atman represented by a man, or vice-versa? Jungian psychology postulated that each individual had elements of the opposite gender—the anima and animus. In the end they decided that ideally it would be best for dramatic purposes if the actor playing an atman should be the same sex as the person she was linked to, and would wear similar wardrobe, though of course this was not possible as the actors numbered three women and four men.

Veronica was less taken by the Hindu philosophy than by the element of consciousness which observes itself. She was more in tune with the Buddhist idea of the abandonment of the self. The technique they developed had an eerie, alienating effect which made her think that the work she was doing was more than just entertaining an audience. It had a mysterious personal meaning. She just couldn't place it.

There was also an unforeseen consequence. Each actor was paired with another, and they always played each other's atman. Except Daniel—he never had one. This pairing created a bond. They didn't just pretend to observe each other, they actually did, with a very focused intensity. That was part of the original idea they had hashed out between them. The result was a closeness—not exactly a merging of selves but a lowering of defences and removal of boundaries. The atman-technique was occasional, not constant, and was partly limited by who had to be where, when.

Rose was getting impatient.

"Okay. Does everybody think they're ready?"

Veronica took her place on stage and Cordelia followed her up, already watching her closely. Raoul took off to the wings which were two thick, black velour drapes flanking the stages. Behind these curtains was another kind of theatre, in which the actors and audience were one. This was where they would wait for their cues, change costumes and joke around with each other. They'd smoke weed, snort whatever was available and engage in some quick sex for sheer pleasure. The pleasure was heightened because they knew that there was a roomful of people out there who were clueless as to what was going on in front of them.

"Action!"

Veronica pottered about with her back to the auditorium until she heard Raoul step on to the stage and she turned to greet him. Cordelia was two feet away, still as stone.

"Oh hello Mr. Spade. Please come in."

Raoul took off his hat and handed it to her. She held on to it for a moment until she found somewhere to put it. She was flustered. At least that's what she wanted him to think. She briefly glanced sideways at Cordelia who stared back into her eyes unblinking. She shuddered.

"Please excuse the mess. I haven't quite settled in." She moved around the stage and took a coat off one of the two armchairs that faced each other. Raoul sat down.

"Mr Spade, I... I... What I told you yesterday wasn't exactly the truth."

"We didn't think it was, Miss… er… so what is your real name?"

"O'Shaughnessy, Bridget O'Shaughnessy."

"Well Miss O'Shaughnessy, we knew you weren't telling the truth but your dollars didn't lie."

"What do you mean?" Veronica sat down opposite Raoul and leaned towards him.

"You paid us too much for being honest but just enough to make that okay."

"Wait, stop… Stop!" Rose had sprung from her chair and was pacing around in front of the stage.

"Sam. Don't try to be Humphrey Bogart. You're not him. This story was a book before it was a movie. And now it's a play. A magical sliver of reality, and you are ruining it by being a caricature. Just be yourself. You are Sam Spade. Forget about Bogart. Now pick it up where you left off."

Veronica was a little thrown and it took a moment to get back into character. She wasn't averse to criticism but this seemed unfair to Raoul. Of course their interpretation had been influenced by the film. How could it not be?

"Do you think this was all my fault, Mr. Spade?"

"Well you told us what Thursby was like. I don't think you were to blame."

"That helps. Thank you."

The lights on the right stage began to come up.

Daniel was measuring a piece of siding. Then he cut it with a handsaw. He was holding it up, about to nail it in place when the two police officers from *The Maltese Falcon*, Lieutenant Dundy and Sergeant Polhaus came out of the wings.

"Hey Buddy, you ever see this guy?" Dundy was holding up a photograph. Daniel peered at it.

Veronica turned in her seat and moved a little closer to Raoul.

"Poor Mr. Archer. Yesterday he seemed so…

"Cut it out. He knew the risks he was taking"

Daniel took the photograph from Dundy and studied it for a minute.

"Who is he?"

"Was, pal. He was. That's Thursby. Floyd Thursby. You sure you ain't seen him around here?"

Cordelia stood behind Veronica's chair, a little to the side. Veronica could feel eyes boring into her head. They weren't judging her but they made her aware of the guilt she needed to feel.

"Did he have a wife? Children?"

"A wife, yeah. She didn't like him that much. No children and a big fat insurance policy."

"What do you do for a living?" Dundy took back the photograph.

Raoul leaned back and tugged gently at his lower lip with thumb and forefinger. He couldn't completely forget Bogart, no matter what Rose had said.

"This is not the time to think about that. There's an army of cops and D.A.'s out there, snooping around."

"You didn't tell them about me, did you?"

Dundy and Polhaus flanked Daniel. He found them threatening. They were the people who were going to send him to 'Nam.

"Well, what do you think? I'm an actor."

"Don't get sassy, kid."

The policemen left looking dissatisfied. Daniel nailed up the plank. He hit each nail three times—the first to set it, the second to drive it and the third to finish it. Every nail was the same. There was a calm, confident rhythm to it that Veronica couldn't help noticing. The experience he obviously had with carpentry seemed out of place with someone so young. He was just a kid really. It never ceased to surprise her, even though he had been doing it almost every night for the past year. The rhythm of his hammer wafted into *The Maltese Falcon*.

"I haven't told them yet. I was waiting to see you first."

A woman with a shopping cart made her way through the auditorium muttering to herself. She parked the cart in front of the stages and looked around her, then her eyes set on Daniel.

"Got a cigarette honey?"

Daniel was reaching for another plank. "No."

She looked as if she was about to move on but then paused, turning towards Raoul, Veronica and Cordelia.

"What are they doing?"

Daniel looked up, "Who?"

"You're not one for words, are you?"

By this time Frank and Len had made their way through the wings, behind the screen, and up the other side to take their places on the left stage. In a performance they would have pulled robes over their shabby suits. In *The Maltese Falcon* they also played Joel Cairo and the Fat Man, respectively. And Len doubled as Brahmā, with his five heads—four after he lost one to Shiva, played by Raoul. The heads were held up by an ingenious harness adapted from football shoulder pads, which could easily be put on or taken off. All of the actors in the ensemble were used to changing wardrobe at breakneck speed.

When the lights came up, they were both sitting in meditative poses. Then Frank spoke.

"First Brahmā created himself. And then everything else. All created from his mind."

"You renting out rooms in this place when you're done?" The bag lady was trying to look past him into the house. Daniel was annoyed.

"I'll never be done."

Frank stared out into the audience.

"He wasn't satisfied with making things from his mind. That's why he told us to come up with a new mode of creation."

The bag lady found a cigarette end on the ground and lit it up.

"You're full of shit."

"You can protect me, can't you? So I don't have to talk to anyone." Veronica was summoning the helplessness she sometimes felt. Raoul was merciless.

"Maybe. But you've got to explain what's going on."

Then Len finally stirred.

"That's how sex came into existence."

Veronica suddenly rose from her chair and walked across the stage, her back to Raoul, giving her voice a little flutter.

"I can't. Not now."

"That's what desire is—the push and pull between the mind and what is outside of it." Len was looking pleased with himself, as if he had just discovered a truth.

Daniel went into the house. He came back out with the drill and started it up.

"Cordelia! Cordelia!" Rose was shouting and waving her arms. The drill sputtered to silence.

"What are you doing up there?"

"I'm playing Bridget's atman."

"What are you doing that for? This is not an atman scene. It has to be intimate. Private."

Cordelia and Veronica looked at each other.

After the rehearsal they sat around and discussed their work and how they could make improvements. It was their customary way to wrap up the proceedings. They took turns to speak. Rebecca spoke first. She played Effie, Spade's secretary and *Sat*, Shiva's wife in 'The Sacrifice'. She was also the bag lady who picked arguments with Daniel when he was building his house, and flouting their communal decision about gender, she played atman to Len.

Leonard Mankiller was as striking as his last name, which seemed to have been a tribal title among his Native-American forbears. He was handsome and had a remarkable ability at repartee like Oscar Wilde. Once someone had dropped a coffee cup that shattered on the floor. He had come back with— "Rose's IUD must have fallen out" before the shards had even settled. He was unabashedly and flamboyantly gay.

Rebecca looked earnest, "I think we've got to be careful with the monologues in 'The Sacrifice'. They verge on being didactic. If it wasn't for the cross-dialogue, they'd be pretty boring." Of all the actors, she was the one most uncomfortable with that play and always commented on it.

When it came to Veronica's turn to speak, she was hesitant. She knew she was about to say the wrong thing, but she said it anyway.

"I wonder about the drill. It seems counter-productive to me. I mean… if dialogue is such an integral part of a play, then why make it inaudible? And frankly the noise is so unpleasant I think we'll lose our audience. It makes no sense."

"Makes no sense?" Up till then, Rose had been unusually quiet, and now it looked as if she wanted to say more but no words came. She stood there with her jaw hanging open, as if teetering on a precipice. Suddenly she grabbed a toaster from the mountain and flung it at Veronica. It hit her on the shin, instantly causing a deep gash which spouted blood. Veronica was stunned. There was no pain, just a flowing of time. She sat looking at her leg as if it did not belong to her but knowing that it did. There was a disconnect, something ruptured within.

Len leaped to her aid. He had found some gauze and gently pushed her back, cradling her leg and raising it to slow the blood loss. He wound the bandage around her shin and calf. Daniel had found some gauze too but Len beat him to it. Fabian came down and led Rose away. "What a life he must have," Veronica thought.

Somehow she managed to get through the performance that night, and as it progressed so did the knowledge that this would be the last. It wasn't just the act of violence, or Rose's predictable unpredictability—her illness in fact. It was more as if the wound were a window. When she looked inside she saw her life in the company—a life that she had once thought was so rich and fulfilling but now seemed tawdry and limited. When she looked outward she saw a clear blue sky with invisible possibilities. She knew it was to the sky that she must go.

During the intermission she went out among the audience as

she always did to ply her trade. She saw herself as a seductress and whore. It was funny how that word 'whore' could be so demeaning to a woman when spoken by a man. That same word in her own thoughts was much more mysterious and eternal, rooted somehow in the carnal, subterranean currents of life. It made her think of the sacred prostitutes of ancient Corinth, with arrows carved into the undersides of their sandals, leaving a direction for strangers to follow in the dusty ground. Her trade in this case was reading fortunes which she thought up off the top of her head, and for which she charged wildly different prices at whim. There was also a little pickpocketing on the side for the thrill of it. The seventy-five dollars a week that she was paid by the company was simply not enough to live on.

Much later, long after the performance was over, there was a party on the sixth floor. Veronica went up there with Len. Daniel said he would come too but changed his mind at the last minute. Since the incident with the toaster, something had changed in Veronica and it made him uncomfortable. She seemed distant and more interested in Len, even though he was gay.

The place was filled with smoke and the hubbub of people talking loudly over each other. There was quite a crowd, jammed together, some dancing, some just standing or swaying. The music struck a strange new reality in Veronica's mind, equally calming and exhilarating. Unexpectedly they came upon Janis Joplin with a wide grin on her face and a bottle in her hand. She must have just come from her gig at the Fillmore East. She looked Veronica up and down, and then down and up. "Nice stuff," she said, her grin getting wider.

Basking in the glow of Janis' words she turned and looked up at Len.

"I'm done, Len."

"I know you are," was all he said.

Dawn was about to break.

Son of Neptune

Simon Bearde, a steward on the *SS Pandora*, made a discovery just as his vessel had passed over the equator into the Southern Hemisphere. The crossing of the line celebrations had lasted two days. Though they were not as violent as they had once been on naval ships, they still had dangerous undertones. It was a kind of maritime Saturnalia where discipline was allowed to lapse as the officers looked on.

On an ocean liner like the Pandora, the ceremony was staged as entertainment and the crew found themselves mummers for the passengers, who needed to be relieved from the boredom that luxury afforded.

Being a griffin, as he had never before crossed the equator, Simon Bearde was taken below and blindfolded before being led back up by two shellbacks to face King Neptune, played by Dr. Gainsborough. His blindfold was removed and Simon could see the water dripping from the doctor's matted wig. He held a trident in one hand and at his side stood Davy Jones, who was Malcolm Curry, a fellow steward and shellback. Curry was a good choice for Davy Jones. He had a pallid complexion and jet black hair. His nickname was The Count. He tended to stand very still and stare, with eyes as dark as his hair—a kind of predatory inquisitiveness.

Curry had a side business which involved selling merchandise from the bond, once he got ashore in Liverpool—alcohol, tobacco, watches, perfume. He was so successful in this venture that he was able to pay a junior rating to do his job while on board.

These activities filled Martin Rice with scorn. Rice was yet another steward. There were a lot of them on the Pandora, whose purpose was to see to the needs of the passengers. He stood at Neptune's right, dressed as the beautiful Amphitrite. The care that he had taken with his costume and make-up hinted at another side to Rice, one which Simon had never imagined.

Both of them were an ongoing joke with the rest of the crew. Curry and Rice—who couldn't get along. It never tired.

When he had first started his job on the ship, he had been clearing some glasses from a table in the lounge, and felt someone's eyes on the back of his neck. He turned to see Curry gazing at him from across the room.

"What's your racket then?"

"What do you mean?"

"Everyone has a racket. What's yours?"

If he had a racket he would never divulge it to a stranger. That would be stupid.

They became friends but Simon never lost his wariness. He was alone on this boat, no matter how many people surrounded him.

Curry had the ability to seem to appear from nowhere, or to be omnipresent. Simon would find himself the object of that steady, searching and slightly tilted gaze.

"Are you coming down for a draw then Si? You soft twat."

They would go to an unoccupied cabin with a half dozen other crew members, each with a few cans of beer. Someone would throw a towel across the crack at the bottom of the door—an act that was more symbolic than effective. Then they would drink the beers and smoke huge spliffs. Soon the stench of marijuana would waft through the bowels of the ship. No one seemed to care. If the authorities were going to make a move on them, they would know, from a cryptic tapping of pipes. By the time the officers arrived they would be long gone. Just like a prison ship, Simon thought—never play cards with these people.

When he stood before King Neptune and his blindfold was removed, the Doctor asked him for his name, which was duly noted in a book by his assistant Davy Jones. Martin Rice stood by, looking lascivious.

"How old are you lad?"

At least his mouth wasn't daubed with shit every time he spoke, as it might once have been on a sailing ship. But he was required to kiss the baby.

The baby was the beer-swollen belly of the chippy, smeared with some unpleasant tasting lotion. A hand on the back of his head pushed him down. He was aware, behind him, of a select group of passengers sitting on deck chairs, drinking gin and tonics served to them by the Purser. Some of them found the proceedings quite amusing. Then he was suddenly flipped backwards into the swimming pool. When he surfaced spluttering, he was immediately ducked by two shellbacks and given the baptism of the line. Then he was hauled out and presented with a certificate splashed in brine, affirming his initiation as a shellback, listing his ship, the date and longitude of his crossing, and instructing all creatures of the deep to refrain from doing him harm. He stood by as the next candidate was led up from below.

The following night a storm raged. He was off duty and lay on his bed listening to the terrifying noises of the ship and watching his jacket that hung from a hook on the wall. There was nothing to do. He could not sleep. He could have sworn that his jacket had just made a full rotation on its peg as the bow smashed down violently, filling the ship with ominous metallic sounds. He had been through storms before and always doubted his survival. Borrowed time was being reclaimed, excruciatingly drawn out over hours until the inevitable breaking point would be reached. Until then, all he had was a morose resignation—nothing to do but wait. It was the same for the passengers, referred to by the crew as 'bloods', but worse for them perhaps, as they didn't have their sea legs. Before his shift had ended he had strode through the lounge, dirty mop in hand. The bloods went through stages of resignation. At first they had tried to resist the storm with drunkenness. Then had come the puking—hence the mop, and finally they had crumpled into silence, ashen-faced, huddled in their own vomit and no longer caring. It had happened quite quickly.

When he got off duty, he thought he would go up and get something to eat. A sudden plunge of the bow caused him to fall upstairs. It was a surprising reversal of gravity that gave him some pleasure, despite his fear.

There were only two other people in the galley. He helped himself to some sliced turkey and mashed potatoes and sat alone at the other end of the table.

"Hey matey. Pass the sauce."

He reached for the bottle in front of him but a sudden precipitous roll sent it careening into an open palm causing a gleeful chuckle.

Back in his cabin, Simon took off his white steward jacket, hung it up and reached for a book. He liked to read when his shift was over, usually popular science books and particularly those on biology. They satisfied his curiosity and inspired it simultaneously. He had no idea how he had ended up a steward. He had always assumed he would achieve more. There was a disconnection, a lack of conviction in cause and effect, or an odd mode of communication between the hemispheres of his brain. Still there was nothing wrong with stewards. Davy Jones didn't care who you were or what you did. It was all the same to him.

The rolling and pitching and the incessant noise prevented him from concentrating and he put down his book.

He wondered what the Old Man was doing now, the man who was responsible for the vessel and the people it contained, respected sometimes begrudgingly for the weight he bore, and often murmuringly criticized for his personal foibles. They say he was fond of a tipple. Was he cowering on his bed, watching his jacket, with the blue and gold epaulets?

That was when Simon Bearde began to make a discovery in his unusual, roundabout way.

The jacket on the hook, potentially turning a full circle, reminded him of a ship's propeller.

Thoughts came to him like strangers on the street, unknown quantities with mysterious provenance. He was unaware of the connections he made. It was as if someone else was thinking and putting the thoughts into his head. He had no clue what would come next. Every idea was a discovery. Other people might have thought these discoveries inane. That was the barrier of separation.

Simon lay on his bed wondering why propulsion often seemed to involve a turning motion—at least in machines. It might relate to a natural expediency like hexagonal cell structure. Then he imagined horses with engines and wheels. A wheel flipped ninety degrees became a propeller. This lumbering, metal whale which clanked and squealed around him was driven through the ocean by two of them, powered by steam turbines.

Bacterial species with prokaryotic flagella transport themselves with a rotary, proton-fuelled motor, which to all intents and purposes powers a propeller, turning in an anti-clockwise direction.

So who was mimicking who? The ship the bacteria, or the other way around? Perhaps there was no cross-talk, though he suspected that there was. Either way, he came to see that humanity with its motor driven vessels was playing the same game as the bacteria, and that cancers, sleeping sicknesses, hemorrhagic fevers, cholera, polio, tuberculosis and all other diseases were in fact treatments or medications whose aim was to stabilize, control and ultimately eliminate the parasite. They were administered from a level as far removed from humans, as humans were from bacteria, a distant level that occupied the same space. Life was parasitical in nature.

Simon found himself swinging his legs from the bed and reaching for his jacket with the noise of the storm in his ears.

What made him step out on to the deck when he knew it

was expressly forbidden, he could not say. Once outside, he was unable to differentiate sea and sky. The only thing that existed was a malevolent force. He hadn't been on deck for more than two minutes, when a great wave crashed over the ship, picked him up and hurled him into the ocean. He didn't even see it. Moments later, the same wave, or perhaps another which followed it, plucked him from the sea and threw him back on to the deck where he had just been standing. No one witnessed it and people were skeptical when he told them later.

But at least he knew that he was lucky to have become a shellback the day before. Being a Son of Neptune had advantages.

The Man in the Dressing Gown

He didn't exactly understand what he was doing.

He stood before the Barber stone. He might have been standing behind it. This was a matter of interpretation or perspective—both of which occupied his professional thoughts.

He liked to wander alone around this large ring of stones with an old village plunked down in its midst. It was calming and meditative, a place for contemplation. The multiple histories of such an ancient site held more gaps than facts—negative echoes which were fecund in their silence.

He was more dreamer than analyst. But there was room for all types at Granger Park. The old mansion was not far from Avebury. It had been the seat of the Smith-Hawkins family whose last remaining member, Sir Edward, had bequeathed it to the state in the 1970s. Some twenty-five years later, the state had sold it to the Russian oligarch Dimitri Evgenev and it was now the Plesky Institute for the research and development of artificial intelligence.

He was lucky to have a job that interested him. Artificial Intelligence encompassed many different fields. His area of focus was the creative field, which included artificial intuition, and what he liked to think of as artificial imagination. Both were concepts that required machines to have consciousness. The general aim of AI was to recreate or simulate the human mind. It was a long road to that goal, with many obstacles—philosophical, technical, ethical and otherwise.

The whole thing was problematic though, as human consciousness was not clearly understood. There had been definitions, hunches, partial comprehension, but no one could say exactly what it was, or if it was exactly anything. Obviously that posed the question of how you could imitate something without knowing what it was you were trying to imitate. Unless the attempt at simulation revealed knowledge of its subject. In which case, putting the cart before the horse might pay off.

But if you were to create consciousness in a machine, why would it have to be human and not something else? There was an ingrained anthropocentrism in the idea that annoyed him. It was natural enough that people measured everything by their own attributes to the extent that it shaped their thoughts. It was a limitation that must be surpassed. He desired a consciousness so alien that it would be impossible to imagine or understand.

Instead of a clump of sod on the ground, he had stumbled upon the evolution of a deity.

At Granger Park he spent much of the day at his computer with figures and statistics. It was a relief to come out to Avebury and exercise his eyes by looking into the distance. He also liked to view the stones from varying degrees of proximity—the shapes against the sky and the mottled, lichened grooves. All around him was evidence of decay. It was a natural process that had romantic overtones which he found appealing. There was a sweetness to decay—foul at times.

As he stood by the Barber stone he decided to imagine how an artificial consciousness might break free from its anthropocentric origin. He was not trying to come up with answers or to solve problems as he did at work. In the real artificial world, Deep Learning would be involved. Such a machine would have to teach itself to forget what it had learned from its autodidacticism. This was more of a poetic exercise. His eyes wandered over the surface of old stone. He could hear birds. Then he looked inwards and began to form a vision of another man.

He wore a dressing gown of pale mustard which some would describe as camel. The cuffs were the colour of cobalt and were trimmed with golden rope. He extended an index finger and ran it over the astrolabe. This specimen was made in Isfahan circa 1749.

He always took breakfast before getting dressed. Black coffee from a silver pot and two slices of toast with butter. The same every day, brought to him by his man Edwards.

This meagre fare was consumed with a rich attention to detail. He sat facing South-East. The gimballed bronze mirror, mounted from the ceiling in one corner of the room bounced the sunlight directly into his eyes on cloudless days, making it hard for him to read, which was a good thing. Reading should not be easy. And reading was what he liked to do in the mornings. The first cup of coffee was taken piping hot, the following three were progressively more tepid. One piece of toast was eaten over the course of an hour, the other left untouched. The meal was interspersed with sips from half a glass of whisky, which he poured himself after Edwards had gone upstairs to lay out his clothes.

Morning was the time of day he felt most free. It was beautifully undefined beneath the comforts of ritual and allowed him to drift aimlessly.

He had risen before dawn, when it was still dark. He liked to be up before the birds. It was a game he played with them, of which they were unaware. Edwards and Evelyne were still in their beds dreaming, as he pulled on his dressing gown and tied a bow in the cord around his waist. Then he went outside, barefoot.

He wandered past the statues that stared unconsciously at the mist hanging above the lawn. The gravel pricked the soles of his feet. He was sixty-seven years old.

With a hesitant leap, he landed in the grass at the bottom of the steps. The grass was long, the lawn was a field. No one cut it any more. He didn't venture out, but merely looked. It was a forbidden land these days, somewhere from which there was no return. He used to wander over the lawn often, when Jakes, the gardener, was still alive and the grass had not reached waist height.

Forty years earlier he had discovered a patch of small button-capped mushrooms in the shade below one of the old oaks. Experimentation with these mushrooms had led to the birth of Edwards, after one strange night in Evelyne's bed. She had been a maid then. After some awkward reshuffling she had become the cook. She had remained in this position ever since, without displaying any particular talent for it, which is why he only ate toast in the mornings. Since that night, when he had made love to a woman who changed shape in his arms, Evelyne had become more disapproving with each passing year. He had been changed too. A promising youth who had brimmed with the expectations of other people, became a disappointment to them. Their unvoiced opinions that he had no substance caused opportunities to wither. Eventually all expectation was abandoned. His life settled into a slow decline, inching towards its culmination. When he considered it, he felt that there was an external force at work, because his own experience was mirrored in that of his family. It was the experience of decline, a cone receding into a point that vanished.

It had once been an influential and powerful family, offering up its members to positions of prestige in every field throughout history, dating back to the feudal era. He remembered as a boy the weekend parties, when eminent scientists, artists, bohemians and aristocrats would sit at the large table, now covered with a mildewed cloth. He was allowed to be present, to listen to the conversations but was discouraged from speaking himself. Had he not eaten those mushrooms, he might perhaps have read Mathematics at Cambridge. He could have spent his days with Bayesian probability, while indulging in long and delicious naps. Now there were only the three of them in this dilapidated manor house, forgotten, and no longer belonging to the world.

He did not mind. At this stage in life his main concern was to follow his thoughts before the grave swallowed him. It was waiting in the mausoleum across the lawn. He would go there before too long, to join the remains of his parents and his only sibling.

He had watched his son grow from a lonely, bereft child to a manservant, without ever knowing that it was his father he served. Edward was a family name. The 's' at the end was an afterthought.

As he continued his breakfast, he read about stone circles. It was a sunny day and the words had disappeared from the pages, which were burned out to a blank white. He put down the book and sipped his cold coffee. He thought of Avebury Circle. He had always been fond of it. Unlike Stonehenge it had not yet become completely victimized by its own fame. Not too long ago, twelve years perhaps, he had visited Avebury. It had been his last excursion. Since then, he had decided to turn inward and the only journeys he made now were to different parts of himself.

He leaned back in his chair, inclining his head up to the mirror. The sunlight bathed his closed eyelids, creating dots and splashes of colour. A suffusion of warm pink broke into spatters of India ink, then expanded into a shade of blue, pure as the sky. That colour filled him with enjoyment, but it did not last. No sooner had he registered his pleasure, than it fragmented into dark globules that danced back again to pink.

As hard as he tried, he could not remember a single detail from his last visit to Avebury. He recalled the stones but he suspected that they were a previous memory. He had first been there when he was seven years old. This last visit would have been his third.

The obvious explanation was that there had never been a memory because he had never made the trip. But obvious explanations had little relevance to him. Since that night, forty years earlier, the boundaries between himself and the rest of the world had become porous. The difference between what he did and what he imagined he did was not clearly discernible. He was aware of himself as an intelligence but he might have been one of those old oaks in the copse across the lawn. He could not even be certain that he existed. He might only be a thought. His third visit to Avebury was more thought than memory.

Harcourt had held open the door to the Daimler as he swung his legs out and stood up to stretch. He had told his chauffeur to give him a couple of hours and then come back to meet him at the same place. Harcourt could loiter in the village and have a smoke, or do whatever it was he did to pass the time.

The village at the centre of the circle irritated him. Why build a village there and ruin a perfectly good site? The view without it would have been spectacular. It was one of the largest stone circles anywhere. He would prefer not to think about it. The village was gone as far as he was concerned.

The grass rippled in the breeze and exuded what he presumed to be the smell of summer. His houndstooth suit was getting too big and was not as comfortable as it had once been. The belt around his waist was tied in a knot, the holes no longer useful. He strode out from the centre, toward the stones. As he approached, he saw that they were widely spaced teeth in a state of advanced decay. Much of that must have been due to the work of Stonekiller Jackson with his sledgehammers and his bad habit of feeding sugary morsels to the giants at bedtime.

He would find the Barber Stone and look at it for a while and then he would have Harcourt stop off at Silbury Hill on the way out. It was a good thing this mound had been built near the road.

He was familiar with the shape of the Barber Stone, vaguely reminiscent of a right ear and apparently named after the barber-surgeon who had been accidentally buried beneath it. The stone was looming up before him. The sight of someone behind it was unsettling.

He took an instant dislike to this young upstart who seemed to be paying him more attention than was courteous for a stranger. He had thought himself to be alone. He was going to have to make some changes. He realised that he didn't need any of this. Not the toast, not the mausoleum, not the astrolabe. None of it. But how to get rid of it?

The answer must lie in dreaming. He had often wondered about his life-long inability to dream. It had seemed to him a kind of psychic constipation. For him sleep meant turning off a machine. For others it was an uninhibited escape from reason. He had never felt particularly constrained by reason, though he could feel its weight. It bound intelligence to paved roads. It might be dressed up attractively to look appealing like some French brassiere. All for the sake of survival perhaps. True survival was to be released, to undress, to shed one's humanity. That night-flight was the one thing that allowed people to return to the life of the guided tour with their sanity intact. It was the balance of a stable oscillation. He could do without the oscillation and stay there always, but he had yet to experience it.

"You should learn some manners young man—staring at me like that."

But the young man had gone, which was as it should be. Now it was time to find Harcourt.

On the drive back to Granger he was filled with excitement and a low level of anxiety. He had been unsuccessful in his attempted escape from anthropocentrism. Yet he had dreamed while awake. He had always regarded dreams as mental analogs, created by the brain from memories, emotions and anything else available internally when deprived of external sensory input while sleeping. But this time he had been in full control of his external perceptions. He had not been asleep. The man he had met seemed as real as he did. He could regard himself as the demiurge who had created this apparition, but he could not infallibly deny that it might just well have been the other way round.

One thing was apparent. If there was to be any valid form of artificial consciousness, machines would need the capacity to dream.

Seven Cries of Delight

Three horses cantered across the plain—a grey Arabian, a palomino and a roan. The dust from their hooves rose up from the ground and dispersed around them. Their riders wore space-suits, the kind used in the Apollo missions of the 1960s. But this was not the moon.

The horses and their riders were headed toward the old farm-stead that had been repurposed. Twenty-four sensors, mounted on poles, looked out towards the plain. No agricultural labour had happened here for generations.

Inside the building, in a quiet room with southern exposure, a few people sat in chairs that had been arranged to face away from each other—a design of communal privacy. Each one of them was immersed in a book. The wires from the electrodes on their temples were neatly twisted and disappeared through a hole in the floor. Enough slack was provided to permit move-ment. A small dog ran around the room, largely ignored by the other occupants.

Outside on the verandah a woman held binoculars to her eyes. They were powerful ornithological binoculars. She trained them on the approaching riders, seeing the sky reflected in their visors, beautifully distorted in the curved surfaces. The reflec-tions looked so vivid. Stratocumulus clouds filled her vision.

As the riders approached she was able to see them with her naked eye, taking in reflection and subject simultaneously, as if looking at a painting of a painting. With their spacesuits glar-ing white in the sun, they passed her by at a gallop and quickly receded into the distance.

The woman sighed and picked up the binoculars again from

the railing where she had left them. She scanned the horizon, wistfully hoping she would see a thylacine and knowing it would be very unlikely. She had not yet managed to climb out from under the destructive weight of an early morning argument. The clouds had helped and a thylacine would put her completely at ease. But there were no thylacines, not even one. There had been reports of sightings, as of yet unsubstantiated, but this was the wrong continent.

Accepting that her disappointment was inevitable, she set down the binoculars again and went inside, through the kitchen to the South Room where the readers, two men and one woman, were engrossed in novels. She knew what they were reading. She had made the selections herself: *A Glastonbury Romance* by John Cowper Powys, *The Hearing Trumpet* by Leonora Carrington, and *My Life in the Bush of Ghosts* by Amos Tutola.

Enough time had now lapsed for her to check on the effect of this reading. To allow time to pass was the reason she had stepped out on the verandah in the first place. She made her way quietly through the room so as not to disturb the readers, fondled the little dog's ears, and opened the door at the far end with the demure confidence of a professional.

The opened door revealed a staircase that led down to the basement. She closed it with barely a click. The basement was not part of the original structure. It was an addition. She passed through the section where the vintage electronic instruments were stored. They were all in impeccable condition.

There was a display cabinet containing Moog synthesizers. There was a Minimoog, a Moog Satellite, a Sonic Six, a Micromoog, a Polymoog and a Moog Taurus.

Another cabinet contained Arps—ARP Little Brother, ARP Odyssey, ARP 2600 and an ARP Explorer. There was also an RCA MkII and three theremins.

The instrument collection had a gravitas. It felt like walking through a chapel. There was a nobility in the latent possibilities of yesterday's analog technologies and her respect was genuine.

She paused among the cabinets, feeling an affinity for these instruments that were never played and rarely looked at. They caused her to wonder about the meaning of collections. That meaning must lie in numbers greater than zero or one, because a collection of one thing seemed extremely unlikely. A collection of nothing could not be considered a collection. This led her to consider numbers less than zero. They would imply a negative collection, such as an art collector with no paintings. There might be a catalogue of all the pictures he did not own, some of them yet to be painted.

It occurred to her that these instruments in their dusty cabinets mirrored the negative collection that was not upstairs. In so doing, they were a perfect representation of meaninglessness. And that meaninglessness might be the same thing as hyper-meaning.

She suddenly made an effort to cease this speculation. It was a direction, that was all. A direction that might lead anywhere, and not necessarily where she wanted to go. These were not the questions she should answer, even if she could.

She moved away from the synthesizers to yet another door. Winter was officially over and Pater would probably be awake. This meant that things could get difficult.

When she opened the door, Pater was standing in the frame, blocking her way. He was old but still strong.

"Women are generally not admitted into this area."

"Oh come on. Don't be ridiculous."

"Well, you'll have to prove you have clearance. I must ask you the questions if you don't mind."

"Go ahead."

"What is the correct time?"

"Time upon a once."

"What happened to the coiled rope?"

"It was forgotten by a sailor."

"From whence came the news?"

"It was delivered by a fly."

"How many totems are necessary?"

"Four and twenty."
"What is to be done with the sum of all things?"
"It is to be divided by seven cries of delight."
The old man begrudgingly stood back.
"Okay. You can come in."

The Sound of the Bridge

I have a large table which seats ten, so when I have the occasional dinner party there are ten guests—usually the same people.

But recently there was a newcomer, Ian Waters. Liz had invited him. He was older than the rest of us. He was seated at the head of the table and I sat next to him.

Though nominally master of my own house I eschewed the custom of taking the head of the table. It was too formal. Maybe I should have got a round table like King Arthur but I didn't have the space for it. Anyway I lived alone so these cumbersome traditions were irrelevant.

Whenever I had people over I always took the chair on the side, next to the head of the table. The occupant of that position always seemed separated from the rest. And that was the case with Ian. There was something odd about him, though I couldn't tell what it was. He seemed normal enough—gracious and friendly, easily engaging in conversation.

Aside from a little small talk, I preferred to avoid conversations at my dinner parties. I would rise constantly from my chair to attend to the food and wine, letting the others amuse themselves. It might seem paradoxical to invite people over and be unwilling to talk to them but I liked it that way. I just listened.

The talk had turned to memory—specifically the idea seemingly corroborated by modern science that in order to recall a memory it had to be reinvented. There was some kind of mechanism involving certain proteins which was beyond me, as I'm sure it was everyone else. But it opened up all kinds of possibilities and questions. If a memory had to be constantly reinvented then was it really a memory? Was it the same each time it was recalled? Maybe there was no such thing as memory. But then what? Could you say that nothing happened?

"Of course things happen."

"But without memory, you can never be sure."

Then Ian began to speak. He had a friend he said, who he would leave nameless. It didn't matter much anyway as none of us knew him. I wondered how he could be so sure of that.

This man he mentioned was a sound engineer. Quite a successful one. He'd had a hand in many records that were probably familiar to all of us.

Ian was a good story teller. That was apparent. Other conversations around the table trailed off as all attention was turned to him.

"He told me that a few months ago he was sitting in his car underneath the Queensborough Bridge in New York, on the Queens side. He had some time to kill and decided to use it by listening to the bridge."

"That's a cool idea."

"Yes. He described to me the sounds he heard. 'Monstrous' was the word he used."

"It's amazing how we can shut out the sounds of the city. We're probably in 'fight' mode all the time without realising it. Can't be good. All that stress and adrenalin."

"Well the sounds he told me about—the screeching and groaning, the banging and the ceaseless roar of traffic had an unexpected effect on him."

"What was that?"

"An image began to form clearly in his mind, seemingly out of nowhere. An image of water. But it wasn't pleasant or relaxing like the ocean crashing on to a beach. No, it was still water, dark and stagnant. Very still. And the thing is, once he had seen that image he couldn't get rid of it. No matter where he went or what he did, it stayed in his mind. Even sleep provided no relief. It infused his dreams.

"After a few weeks this obsession began to take its toll. I met him at that time and that's when he told me what had been going on. He seemed to be in a state of nervous exhaustion, or hyper-anxiety, or whatever it's called these days. He had trouble concentrating and had completely lost his appetite. He said he was going to get medical help.

"He went to a number of specialists and they ran a gamut of tests. Initially they had suspected a brain tumour. He had several MRI's but there was nothing abnormal as far as they could tell. In the end the best they could come up with was that he was suffering from panic attacks. Though, from what he had read about it, he didn't think that his condition fit the diagnosis. It wasn't something that went away and came back. It was there the whole time—an onslaught. They prescribed him some pills to calm him down but the image still remained. It was a good thing he had health insurance as I'm sure it cost a fortune. He had coverage through his wife—the music business is not known for providing benefits. She's done quite well for herself. She is the dean of some prestigious college."

Ian was beginning to lose his thread. The attention around the table faltered. But then I had the feeling that his rambling about doctors and medicine was deliberate. He was using some kind of oratorical punctuation, preparing his audience for what was to follow. He disturbed me. More so because I did not know why.

"Maybe the medication did work after all. It might have calmed him enough to think more clearly. Either way, soon after that he got the idea that this persistent image was a memory that manifested itself in an unusual way. Once he had come to that realisation—if that's what it was, he had a direction to follow and felt some relief. That was short-lived though, because he started seeing a submerged face. Sometimes it was there and sometimes not. Perhaps he saw strands of hair floating in the dark water. If this was a memory, it was not a good one."

Liz interrupted. "What did his wife make of it?"

A flicker of irritation crossed Ian's eyes, but it was momentary, as the passing shadow of a cloud.

"That's complicated. They'd been married a long time but

they'd never got along. I've often wondered why they stayed together. It could be that they both derived some mutual benefit from perpetual disagreement and resentment... Anyway, once he had suspected this image was a memory, he began to search for it. The recurring face haunted him but no matter how hard he tried, he couldn't remember anything.

"We assume without thinking that our memories belong to us. We can recall them at will and make whatever use of them we choose. So imagine his condition. It was a disintegration, an alienation that separated him from everything he thought he knew and left him as a mere object acted upon by a senseless existence.

"Accepting that he had reached a dead end, he took another approach. He tried to enlarge upon the picture—to see more detail, hoping that he would find something that would trigger his memory and that all would be revealed.

"He saw that the water was contained in a rusted metal tank that stood above ground. He looked beyond it and saw trees. Unruly, unkempt.

"It could be an old cistern for collecting rain water, he thought. Somewhere rural. A tank like that might have been the water supply for a cabin in the woods. A hunting cabin perhaps. He realised he couldn't visualize the cabin because as the observer of this image, it would be behind him. But he felt he was getting somewhere at last and wracked his brain for a memory of such a place."

"So tell me Ian, how do you know so much about all this?"

Paddy sat at the other end of the table. He was a nay-sayer, always skeptical, and seemed to enjoy picking holes in other people's statements. I wondered if he had been like that as a child. Ian had met his match, I thought.

But Ian was not thrown. He glanced down the table and countered with "I imagine you are aware of empathy..." Then he picked up where he had left off.

"With a jolt he remembered his wife telling him that her grandparents had owned some land in Greene county. They had built a small cabin, where they would go to escape the summer heat in the city. She had never liked the place. As far as he knew, it was still in the family but he couldn't recall ever going there himself. Still he felt he had found a piece of the puzzle. It was a starting point.

"Maybe it was no coincidence that now he had fixed a location for his vision he saw the body again, face up, just beneath the surface. Pale with strands of hair that gently undulated in the still water as if by Brownian motion. He stared with a growing horror at what was before him.

"With constant, gnawing introspection, he came to the conclusion that he had killed someone and deliberately forgotten about it, or repressed it. That thought, now unleashed, took hold of him with frenetic abandon. He examined his entire life as much as he could remember it, searching for a victim and a motive.

"There had been a time when he was younger when things had been much more volatile. That was when he still believed in what he did and in the products he made. He had lived the life, to the hilt. But it all seemed so murky now, and offered up no clues.

"He was going to have to find that cabin and take a look for himself. That was the only way he would know whether this vision was a repressed memory or not. He would search that tank. He pondered that he might be an unwitting psychic receiving information on another's crime. But that was unlikely—wishful thinking perhaps. His gut told him that he was the culprit.

"He wondered about the best way to get the address. His wife must have it. Should he be straightforward with her, or circumspect? He decided to be honest and tell her what he planned to do. She knew what he had been going through and was probably as exasperated as he was.

"The trouble was, when he asked her one morning before she left for work, she couldn't remember it. She had been a child when she went there last. And she had always hated the place. She didn't even know if it was still standing. Her grandfather had built it and he was a cheapskate.

"In the end, with assistance from relatives, she was able to provide it. The cabin still existed as far as anyone knew.

"He picked a Thursday to drive up there. Days of the week didn't mean much to him, not working an orthodox job, but he wanted to avoid the weekend traffic.

"He travelled light—his GPS, a shovel, wire-cutters, rain gear, a bag of nuts and a gallon of water. As an afterthought he took the pearl-handled revolver, given to him by a music promoter many years before that had languished in a drawer ever since.

"It took just over three hours to get there. Traffic was heavy in the city but thinned out as he drove further North. He found himself on a dirt road leading deep into the woods. It was barely drivable and confused his GPS. Its female voice told him to turn around as soon as possible. But he kept going and reached it at last—if it was indeed the right place.

"He turned off the car and sat for a while. Outside there was a light drizzle. The trees glistened with dampness. Everywhere around him there was decay. It was as prevalent as growth. He was staring at a constant process of death and regeneration and it all appeared completely motionless. It was a similar perception of scale that allowed a person to stand on the world and be unaware of its rotation. The fallen branches and the beds of leaves were striking in their complexity. Everything was rotting.

"He turned his eyes to the cabin in front of him. It was small and appeared to be L-shaped. There was a storm door of corroded aluminium, pockmarked with age and flecked with the white dots of oxidization. As his eyes roved over the building and noticed the mildew creeping up onto the walls from the ground he realised that his powers of observation had become honed. In equal measure his obsessive search for a memory had receded. But that cloying, clawing feeling had been replaced with fear. It was time to do what he had come there for.

"He got out of the car and peered through a small window into the cabin. Widows so minuscule would not be acceptable these days. It made him understand how different life was in the past, and how much was now taken for granted.

"He couldn't see clearly, it was dark inside. He swung open the storm door and tried the main door. It was unlocked. Cautiously he stepped in.

"The first thing he noticed was the strong smell of mould. Immediately to his right was a room. Probably it was once a bedroom. He wondered what people had found to do there all summer. Ahead of him was a short, narrow corridor that led into what he presumed was the kitchen. Beyond that was another claustrophobic bedroom.

"Halfway along the corridor, on the left side, was a closet with an open sliding door. A pile of shoes lay tumbled from it on the floor in a haphazard fashion.

"It was an eerie sight. Why so many shoes in a place like this? They suggested a sudden and unplanned exodus, a moment of panic that had lasted for years. He had a strong sense of those anonymous feet that had once worn those shoes, yet departed without them. What could have caused them to do that? Everything that had happened echoed through time.

"Next to the closet was another door. This was the bathroom. So they hadn't used an outhouse as he would have expected. Maybe the bathroom was added later. He stared in. There was a stained toilet with a cracked seat, and on the wall next to it a metal medicine cabinet with no door. A few cloudy glass bottles still stood on the shelves, connected to each other with spider webs. A bathtub stretched along the other wall, filled with building detritus—broken planks, cardboard and rolls of mildewed wallpaper.

"It didn't take him long to finish his exploration of the cabin, and he was relieved to go back outside. He had been looking for something to jolt his memory, but beyond the shoes and the ubiquitous evidence of mice and spiders, nothing else had caught his eye.

"The jumble of shoes was jarring but it didn't provide him with any of the details he had hoped for, only a disconcerting feeling that just exacerbated his sense of foreboding.

"Outside, the drizzle kept coming. The sky was opaque and oppressive. It kept secrets and gave nothing away. He pulled up the hood of his anorak and walked around to the back of the building.

"And there it was, just as he had seen it. The rusted metal tank sat on a concrete slab about thirty feet away. He hadn't noticed the slab in his vision but the trees were the same. They were smaller than most of the others in the forest. The area had obviously been cleared once and they had been encroaching on it ever since in a gradual but relentless process of reclamation. Broken wood lay scattered randomly across the landscape, like the shoes outside the closet.

"The tank stood about four feet tall. Its rim had corroded away in some areas, leaving jagged holes reminiscent of maps of unknown coastlines.

"With trepidation he peered over the edge. Leaves were suspended in the dark water, clustered in the corners. He was relieved not to see a floating corpse but he knew that he had to be certain, so he went back to the car and got the shovel. He started to churn the water with it but it wasn't long enough to probe the depths. He looked around and found a piece of electrical conduit. It was hard work pulling it out of the ground. Eventually he carried it back to the tank and poked around in the foul water.

"More leaves rose to the surface, dark and slimy, releasing a powerful odour. It was the peculiar and unpleasant smell of things that rot in water. He splashed himself a few times in the process and recoiled in disgust. A dead frog rose up, slowly gyrating. It was bloated and almost translucent.

"At every prod he became more tense, knowing that soon he would come across the person he had killed and then he would have to face himself. Who was this person he had brought here and held down in this water? And why? After years of ignorance he would have to shoulder the responsibility for what he had done. He would stagger beneath it wherever it might lead him, but at least he would know himself. This half-life existence of dream and supposition would be over. It was driving him mad.

"Ten fraught minutes of searching finally convinced him that there was no human body in the tank. He stood back and threw down the pipe. Nothing he had seen explained the image that had plagued him but now he knew that he had not committed murder.

"He turned his back on the tank and walked into the woods. He wanted to see if that wretched vision remained in his mind. It was gone. He had exorcised himself.

"As he aimlessly put distance between himself and the cabin, he felt the anxiety that had consumed him for so long dissolve into the forest. It gave him the sensation of clarity. He was able to see all the recent events in his life and the strands that bound them to each other. The metallic sounds of the bridge, the sounds of inorganic pain, the metal tank, the water it contained, the face beneath the water, the fear and pain and loneliness of drowning. The meaning that lingered in a pile of shoes. The dissipation of all things.

"That feeling of clarity was just a moment. It passed quickly as twigs snapped beneath his feet and brambles snared his clothes. His intentions passed along with it. There was no need to make sense of anything. All that remained was the entropic process of growth and decay.

"Relief takes different guises. For him I think it was a flow-ing-out, an emptying."

Ian sat back in his chair and sipped from his glass. Every-one else relaxed. I had found his monologue overbearing. It seemed to be an unreasonable demand for attention and left me wondering about his purpose, because I was sure he had one. I scraped back my chair and headed for the kitchen. I could hear their voices from my refuge. Paddy was talking.

"Interesting story. But I imagine that's all it is—a story, right?"

I could hear Ian's mellifluous voice in response.

"We were talking about memory. Isn't that just what a memory is—a story, or a series of them?"

"It sounds to me like you were talking about yourself. Are

they your memories you've been telling us?"

That was the other Iain, the one with the extra 'i' in his name. His parents had probably added it in a nod to their Gaelic ancestry. He was someone who always appeared to consider what he was about to say before speaking.

"Well yes, they are my memories but only inasmuch as they are what I remember about someone else's memories. But it's possible that I might just be reinventing them" He chuckled.

"But you went from describing someone else's memories to becoming that person yourself."

"I was telling a story. Isn't that what we do in stories—wear the shoes of our characters? Empathize, as I was saying."

I missed what followed as I had turned on the tap to rinse a glass and it momentarily drowned out the conversation. I was happy to be free of it for a while. It had left me feeling uneasy. Then I heard Jane speaking.

"So what became of your friend? Did he recover?"

"I can't really say."

"What do you mean? You don't know?"

"Well you see he never returned from that trip upstate. Maybe he's in hospital, or perhaps he ran off somewhere and started a new life. I don't know what became of him. But I'm sure he'll resurface sooner or later."

"You don't seem too worried."

"Worry doesn't accomplish much, does it?

And then I heard Paddy chime in again, in his accusatory style.

"Would you say that memories are limited to the past? Could there not be a memory of something that has not yet happened?"

"That would be precognition, wouldn't it?"

"I'm not sure there's a difference."

I came back to the table to clear it. Liz was leaning in towards Ian, looking at him earnestly, conspiratorially almost.

"Haven't you spoken to his wife?"

She struck me as overly concerned about this man's wife.

What was it to her? It annoyed me. All the more so since Ian was her friend and she was the one who had invited him to my house. "You don't mind if I bring a friend along?" She had asked me. "He's an interesting guy."

That might be but he wouldn't be coming back again, as far as I was concerned.

Ian didn't reply straight away. He seemed lost for words, or distracted by his own thoughts. The confidence he had displayed earlier with so little effort, now seemed less strident.

"Spoken to her? Yes of course. We moved in together recently."

The Article

There's a country down the road I read about recently in the newspaper, or more accurately in its digital counterpart. This country has just been discovered. Archaeologists have been working on it for some time but only now can definitively say that what they have been excavating is, or was, a nation state—small, but a nation state nonetheless.

It gets more interesting because this settlement that they insist is a nation state, is almost twenty thousand years old according to their radiocarbon dating.

I would have thought the words—'nation' and 'state' would have been irrelevant twenty thousand years ago. Of course their dating might be false. They could have unearthed something deposited at an earlier time and in their eagerness confused the issue.

Apparently the evidence of civilization lay in a cache of hard clay tablets found beneath thirty feet of silt. These tablets had been stamped with writing by means of movable type equivalent to the early European printing presses of Gutenberg or Caxton.

While reading the article I could not help but think about the established opinion that humans only arrived on this continent around ten thousand years ago. I've often felt this might be wrong but what I was reading now approached absurdity, and as I happen to like absurdity I kept on reading.

The script on the clay tablets was alphabetical. Not only that, it was printed in the Roman alphabet. Furthermore, the language written was English.

The brazenness of it put Piltdown in the shade. It would be as if I walked around claiming to be seven hundred years old, or that the combustion engine did not exist. Could anyone be expected to take this seriously? And if not, what was the point of it?

I was now motivated to discover that point and avidly devoured the rest of the piece. It was written in a pseudo-archaic style that reminded me of the Old Testament. The bulk of it concerned religion. As I started to read I was fearful that it was to be an exposition of some wayward claim about Christianity. I was happy to find that these ancient people had a large pantheon. But then there was a pleasant surprise.

It would appear that none of the citizens of this nation did any kind of work. Instead, most of their time was spent in cajoling the deities. No attempt was made to hide the fact that they had created their own gods—not the other way around as in most creation myths. It was almost a point of pride. The tablets recounted how back in the dusky past their ancestors had assembled this pantheon with the idea of making a super-race of servants.

Problems began soon after the Creation. The gods were a lazy bunch. They were also wily and made themselves scarce. So, to get anything done, the relevant deity had first to be found, then forced, tricked or bribed into carrying out the desired task. It was a full time occupation and theoretically could have led to the demise of this oddly advanced civilization.

I wondered if what I was reading was a parable about the implications of robotics and automation, a retelling of the Frankenstein story, a romantic idea about the dangers of meddling with the processes of nature. An idea which, romantic or not, might have some pertinence.

It could be that people were too clever for their own good, bound forever to opposing cycles of damage and control, of life and death. It made me think of that old image of the serpent eating its own tail, or chasing it.

The codex presented in the clay tablets was part history, part list of names and part instruction manual.

The gods, as super-beings, were strong and intelligent, with the ability to change shape at will. They used these talents to avoid their creators and pursue their own existence with indolence or playful caprice. Their emotional development ranged from toddler to early adolescent, so they were not easy to reason with when found.

> Should you be faced with an insurmountable object, even as you should move a mountainside, any task which requires heavy-lifting, a great weight upon your head, you must set out to find Lankouson. He is the strongest among the Gods but he is loath to pick up the smallest thing. Be not a fool to assault him. Offer him small cakes. Lankouson is hungry for dainty foods. You may also bargain with favours of the body. He has affinity for men and women alike. Look not in his face.

Another passage caught my attention.

> Are you to be plagued by ghosts, ... *(word missing)* ... shadows on the skin. Search you for Meleke. She hides in the rivers and the ... *(word missing)* ... . Meleke is angered by men but she is susceptible to flattery and whimsical speech. Behold her and praise her. Beseech her to dance naked before you.

And:

> When you must calculate, go forth and seek the Goddess Verdu. She will appear in the likeness of a one-armed man riding backwards on a horse. Approach her silently from the head of the beast and snare her with a ... *(word missing)* ... of metal. If she should look upon you she shall become as the morning mist. You will search for her only in the middle of the day. When you have caught Verdu be mendacious and ply her with insults. She desires only that you should treat kindly with her. Thus you must tire her first with lies and harsh words, then present her

with that which must be calculated. Laud her and give thanks upon the answer.

In the sections that dealt with the history of the civilization there were frequent references to borders—called 'edges' in the text—and of those who belonged within them, and of those who did not. There was a long established system of government, which to modern sensibility would be considered a benign dictatorship. There were also public sporting events, races and ball games which were very popular, usually involving the gods as participants and the citizens as spectators. These things, in conjunction with physical evidence of widespread deforestation, deep pits containing household refuse and charcoal mixed in with the soil, led the authors of the study to conclude that they had discovered a nation-state. It even had a name—Vispalon

I always assumed that the concept of 'nation' had begun to coalesce at the end of the medieval era. Though I didn't believe what I read, I wasn't averse to the idea. Erroneous ideas are not necessarily bad. They can exist as theories, which might in turn stimulate other theories. *The Origin of Consciousness in the Breakdown of the Bicameral Mind* by Julian Jaynes postulates a theory that I don't believe but which I like. It is thought provoking.

Every few years skeletal remains are found which make us rethink our dating of early humans or of their arrival somewhere. The wolf/dog evolutionary transformation is now considered to have happened much earlier than previously thought. Not so long ago, the age of the planet was clocked at four or five thousand years. As time passes, things seem to keep happening earlier than before.

It was a long article, utterly nonsensical but quite entertaining. Maybe that was the point of it—news as entertainment—not unheard of. When I had finished it, I decided to look up the principle players. The person who had headed the dig was a Dr Karen Hornesby, affiliated with Ealing University. It was a little uncanny, as I am from Ealing myself, and have never been aware of any university there. One could of course have sprung up after I had left, so I looked into it. There did indeed seem to be an Ealing University, or a University of West London, with campuses in Ealing and Brentford, but of Dr. Hornesby I found no trace. Her colleague, the curiously named Paxton Domingo, a Phd student, was equally enigmatic. So the linchpins of this story didn't exist, or were not who they claimed to be.

The article said that this ancient nation was near where I now live but did not say exactly where. I said it was down the road but I was just being poetic. That left me in the frustrating position of knowing nothing. It was the kind of frustration you feel when you have misplaced something that you suspect is close by. In this case I couldn't say whether it was close by or not. It most likely didn't exist but the feeling was the same.

The only place left to turn was to the organ of democracy. I contacted the paper which had published the article and questioned them about its veracity. I asked them about the subject and the journalist who had reported on it, whose name I can't remember now.

I received a reply in a few days. They had never published that article and suggested that I might be confusing them with another paper, though they were not aware of any such story.

I immediately checked online but of course couldn't find it. They had obviously taken it down. Maybe it was a prank, or a hacking incident.

It was also entirely possible that I had written it myself. But why would I have done that?

Effects and Causes

It was late at night when he got home. The outside light was off and it took a few seconds to find the keyhole. The door creaked open and his hand reached knowingly into the darkness of his house, as if into a glove. Then he felt along the wall for the light switch.

The moment it took for the circuit to be closed and the room to burst into light was the culmination of almost sixty-five million years, perhaps even longer. Ever since the divergence of species from whales to hominids, this event had been lumbering towards its conclusion—the illumination of a room in the middle of the night. Though this might have appeared to be the end of the line, it was not, as conclusions are inconclusive and just a matter of metrology. The important word was 'uncertainty'.

It was with uncertainty that he glanced at the table by the door, now that he could see it. This was where letters accrued. There was also a chessboard, set up but rarely used. He thumbed through the envelopes. Each one was a demand for money. Once he might have found ideas, and descriptions of other places. There might have been a love-letter. He would have recognized the familiar handwriting on the envelope and felt excited as he tore it open. These had been personal words. The bills before him were impersonal. It was sad that such a rich mode of communication had been reduced to a mere vehicle of obligation.

There was another table by a door, in another place at a different time. Along with the letters there was a newspaper. The headline glared at him.

'MAN KILLED IN A CROWD WITH
POISONED UMBRELLA'.

77

It was a case of fiction peeking through reality, as a marble would reveal its shape through a thin layer of rubber. Quite a rare event. The grey zone of spies, usually running parallel, had veered off course and touched his life. That is what made the article so fascinating. Then he became aware that Mrs. B was reading over his shoulder. He turned and saw that she looked agitated and very pale.

"Are you all right?"

"I knew that man."

She hurried out, leaving him to wonder what on earth she had to do with it.

Mrs. B lived upstairs. Beyond that he didn't know much about her. Their relationship was limited to occasional encounters in the shared hallway, usually near the table by the door. Still, the few conversations they had were more profound than flippant small talk and left him with the vague impression that there was something she wished to divulge but could not bring herself to. And why to him, a young man twenty years her junior?

She told him once that a person like him could not exist in her country. It was a brief statement dense with inference. For everything she said, there was more left unsaid. She did not say what country she came from, or what kind of person she supposed him to be.

He assumed she had a husband as she used the title 'Mrs.' which was also on the nameplate outside, but he had never seen any evidence of Mr. B. She seemed to live alone. They were probably divorced. One day, out of the blue, pre-empting a question he might never have asked, she told him that her husband had died some years before, leaving her a widow. So that explained it.

Except that a few months later when they met at the foot of the stairs she said that her husband had been away for a long time. She did not seem to have any recollection that she had told him her husband was dead. Not knowing what to make of it, he had no opinion. Just that there were inconsistencies in what people said to each other. Only later did he give it some thought. She had never said where Mr. B had gone, leaving space enough for speculation. Now, with his eyes and fingers on the bills before him, he realized that she had implied Mr. B was in some foreign city. Budapest? Prague? Or was it a necropolis? The Valley of the Kings perhaps.

The last time they had met, a drawn Mrs. B requested that should anyone come asking for her, he should say that she was not there and that he had not seen her for months.

A few days later he answered the door to two men in raincoats. Had he seen Mrs. B? No he had not. Not for at least three months.

He didn't see her again. She disappeared as completely as if she had never been there, leaving more questions than answers, and nothing resolved. Where did she go? Did she make it? Was she abducted? Was she alive?

Whatever had transpired she must be dead by now, considering his own age.

He let the bills fall back on to the table, where he would leave them until they were no longer current and could be thrown away with impunity, at least as far as he was concerned.

He was alone in the house. His wife had just left him, possibly due to a lack of affection or maybe something else. The bed was empty.

As he sat on the sofa and unlaced his boots it occurred to him that this old trope of cause and effect might actually play out in reverse. In which case the cause of his recent journey was the act of his return five days later. This was much more interesting. Because Mrs. B had disappeared, a man had been killed. Because Mrs. B's husband was dead, he lived in another city. Things were beginning to make sense.

Because he was sleeping, he went to bed.

He woke up with the balmy thought of effect and cause to sustain him. He went down to the basement. A piece of frayed rope caught his eye. It was wedged behind a book on the shelf. He pulled out the book, and there it was—his quipu. He hadn't seen it in years. He had the feeling of entering into a dream as he held it in his hands and examined it. He ran his fingers through the multitude of coloured strings, each one bearing a series of intricate knots. He allowed his fingers to play with them. It was old but still fresh. He knew what it was, though it was so long since he had seen it that it might not have existed before now, and new memories came flooding in.

Such as a trip to Oaxaca. He had been staying in the Spanish colonial part of town, the place where tourists stayed. Every day was spent walking, as happens when you are a tourist with a modicum of curiosity. Every day further and further. The streets were flat-looking, small and low, but glimpses through doorways revealed courtyards that seemed bigger than the buildings that encompassed them. Thick walls from the 16th Century. Lush plants on terraces, bougainvillea brimming with colour. Diego Rivera's house, filled with a collection of strange pre-Columbian artefacts. On every corner stood oddly pubescent police officers, usually in groups of two or three, with baseball caps and blue clothes. He discovered that they were tourist police. It was an unpleasant thought that these people were there to watch foreigners. But then he learned their purpose was to protect them. Beyond the enclave of the old colonial area there was a much bigger town blighted by deep poverty. That was where he went next, and that was where he bought his quipu from an old woman in a market. It cost next to nothing.

The book that had obscured the quipu was a history of numbers. Unity preceded the void. Zero was invented much later than one. The void might well have been behind the bookshelf because the empty space created by the removal of the history of numbers and the quipu revealed a hinge. He imagined it being said that one hinge led to another, and he started to pull books from the shelves until he saw two more. A door. What else to do but open it?

It opened more easily than he had expected. He stood at the threshold and looked in. It was a large room, much bigger than the basement which was the size of what he had once believed to be the footprint of his house. Beyond it he could see entrances to other rooms. The whole area was lit by natural light that filtered in through small windows. Like the basement, it was half underground.

What an incredible piece of luck. It was a mysterious pleasure to discover that there was more to this house—to realise that he knew much less than he had previously assumed. He stepped in, quipu in hand.

The decor was not particularly to his taste but the place was clean despite its air of disuse. Rooms which have not been occupied for years have a curious stillness, affecting the passage of time.

He trod lightly as he explored the other rooms—three in all. A kitchen, a bathroom and an empty room that looked as if it might have been an art studio or a workshop.

He went back to the main room and sat down on the sofa. It was upholstered in a material with a floral design, green in hue. Comfortable enough. He leant back and closed his eyes to get a sense of things.

Soon his thoughts returned to the quipu. Had he bought it, or had it been sold to him? There was a subtle difference, a difference of volition. That woman—she must have been a witch, a Zapotec witch, or shaman. He could see her in an old dilapidated cottage, high on an arid mountain. She has sent her assistant, a young girl, to gather the magical herbs from the countryside. She has a specific way to prepare these herbs. It is arcane. She drinks some of the liquid. Then she sits for hours singing gently, almost inaudibly. She is weaving a web of connections in another world. After that she begins the three-day journey to the marketplace in the town below. She walks with the quipu on her head.

So the old woman had selected him. She knew he would be there. Perhaps she had directed him. She had a purpose for this transaction. He opened his eyes and looked at the knotted rope on his knee. He had no memories of these events and everything had to be created anew. The avenues were wide open. For the sake of simplicity, and perhaps a dash of humour, he could assume that the quipu was in the bookshelf because it was in some ways a book, just not in the western sense of covers and pages and printed words. Braille was a series of bumps to be felt. There was no need for the recording of communication to be limited to the norms of one's own culture. But he was forgetting himself, the bookshelf was there because of what it contained.

As far as he knew, quipus were used by South American peoples, the Incas among them, to record numbers. The coloured strands had meaning. The knots in them had meaning. The distance between the knots had meaning. It was all shrouded in mystery and had no meaning for him at all. And yet...

What do you do if you desire meaning and there is none to be had? You make it.

This quipu he held was a novel. It might involve numbers, but numbers and letters were linked, both being cultural inventions and not inherent. He had started reading it once before but had put it down. Now he would try again, using a different approach—with touch as well as vision.

The flower on the railing had been removed, so there was no way for him to know that things were not going to go according to plan. He took a last sip of coffee and returned the cup to the saucer. Then, glancing at his watch, he got up, pulled his coat from the chair-back and made for the door. Just outside he stopped momentarily to put on his coat, and used the time to scan the street for anything untoward. He let his eyes wander without settling on any one thing. Nothing to distract his attention. The coast was clear. Coat now buttoned, he stepped into the pedestrian slipstream.

This was to be a standard drop, if anything could be considered standard in this business. In fact he would be receiving. He'd done it a hundred times. As he rounded the corner by the department store he would accidentally bump into a woman coming the other way. He would pause barely long enough to apologize and be on his way. The woman he was to collide with was Beatrice. This was not the first time they had done this. In another world he would have asked her out to dinner.

When he reached the corner there was no sign of Beatrice. He slowed to look in a shop window, then kept going. Still nothing, just the normal crowd one would expect at this time on an overcast day. People leaving work, shop girls, businessmen with umbrellas. All of them blissfully unaware of the game being played out in their midst. He could feel himself tense up. Something had gone wrong. But wait... there she was, hair covered in a blue silk scarf. Coming towards him. His heart leapt. But no, it wasn't her. He felt a sudden stabbing pain in his calf. Then a rush of nausea and dizziness. His legs buckled. He was falling...

Philip had called and said that unfortunately he had to cancel their dinner plans. That meant that the drop was off. It left her feeling nervous. It also left her in possession of sensitive material for longer than she had wanted. Why had they aborted? She telephoned the restaurant and cancelled the reservation she had made, as cover, for the benefit of those listening and watching.

It was nerve-wracking working for both sides. Bad enough working for one. Two caused more than twice the trouble. Sometimes she took pride in her situation. She felt a heightened sense of reality and power. The civilians around her floated by like flat characters from a dream. But she also felt like an insect scurrying to avoid being crushed. Spy-craft was a side effect of humanity, it perverted the fundamental aspects of life. How could there be love if there was no trust? How could friendship grow in a bed of suspicion, a bed fraught with twisting and nefarious motives? Work could not be distinguished from leisure, work that was ultimately pointless and only able to exist on the illusion of its own importance. Yet that illusion had concrete effects on the life around it. Her life was entirely corrupted.

That was what she liked about the boy downstairs. He was too naive to be corruptible. She was amused and irritated by his way of life—a kind of teenage rebellion that lashed out at the state that supported him. He was probably collecting money every week for doing nothing. She had lived in this country long enough to understand its workings but couldn't quite shake her own upbringing, feeling a residual disapproval. He simply would not have been allowed to exist. He would have been tailored in a way that was deemed fitting to his abilities and to the benefit of the state. He would have become an engineer, a factory worker, a party official perhaps. And if not, then re-indoctrination or worse. But she also felt a fondness for him for the very same reasons. His innocence was refreshing. She could see him standing quizzically in his tight trousers and ridiculously pointed shoes, leather jacket, no shirt, baby-faced. His lack of awareness was a strength. It protected him from the kind of strictures that bound her. She half-imagined inviting him upstairs. But she would never do that. She did not want to tarnish him.

She thought ruefully about her own husband, her part-time husband who would materialize whenever the need arose for her to be married. It wasn't always the same man. She had been married once, for real, but that was a long time ago.

She didn't have much time. She needed help. But where to turn? The people who had killed Harry would be coming for her next. She had learned about it from reading the young man's paper. It was as if the ground had suddenly caved in beneath her. Why did she learn it from a newspaper and not from a phone call or message? She was being isolated. The drop may have been aborted to set her up. That meant time was short. She could tell the boy was concerned, she could see it in his eyes. The less he knew the better...

He put down the quipu and stretched his legs. He rather liked this book. He would read more. But he felt the desire for some

Lapsang Souchong. He always found the combination of rough smokiness and refined black leaves to be conducive to thought. He would return.

But he never did.

When he went back down to the basement with his mug of tea, he found that the spacious extra rooms, along with his quipu and the rest of the story, were no longer there.

Double Helix

The staircase wound in a clockwise direction so that the man standing at the top, if he were left-handed, which he was, would have greater freedom with his sword-arm than those coming up from below, most likely right-handed and hampered by having their weapons on the inside of the curve.

Things would obviously have reached a critical stage if people were ascending the staircase with swords. It was on such a day, sometime in the late twelfth century that Sir Hugh Berners disappeared from history, taking with him four or five others. It was a left-handed assailant who dispatched him. A possibility he had not taken into consideration when speaking to his architect.

She was left-handed and had an affinity for staircases, especially spiral ones. The staircase she had just discovered only minutes ago at the disused bank where she now found herself, was a perfect specimen. It tunnelled its way up three stories with pleasingly tight curves and a sensuous regularity, light grey in colour, warmed by an amber tone from the skylight above.

She had to go up it.

The bank had become a space which was rented out for functions such as high-end weddings and corporate parties. Today was a day of preparation. She did not have much to do, so exploration was in order.

When she got to the top, slightly winded, she came out on a landing with a railing, from which she could look down on the concourse below. There were two tables with DJ equipment on them, and a mess of jumbled wires. There was also a man up there. He had on a white shirt and black suit. His hair was cut short. He didn't look like a DJ. Security perhaps. She was surprised to run into someone.

"Hi."

"Hello."

His face was unrevealing. He did not introduce himself and nor did she.

"Are you working here with the function?"

"Yes."

"Best get back down then."

He turned away to signify that the conversation was at an end, or to resume what he had been doing. She went back down, faster this time, without the poetry of the ascent but giddiness instead, until her downward momentum thrust her stumbling through the little door into the room below.

†

Trouble began in earnest for Sir Hugh when he set off on the Third Crusade. Full of Christian zeal, he had stopped in Rome on his way to the Levant. There, in a bout of drunkenness, he had slept with an illegitimate daughter of the pope. Though the pope denied having any children, excommunication caught up with Sir Hugh just as he was embarking on the siege of Acre.

Atrabilious by nature, Hugh took to his tent and refused to fight. While he sulked morosely in the heat, a vengeful anger overcame him, untempered by the words of others because he would not deign to converse.

†

"Deirdre, where were you? I've been looking for you."

Violet Myron, known half-affectionately behind her back as Quag, was the Producer and the woman in charge. She was perfectly aware of her nickname, just as she was of most things. Details were her playing field. She had her usual air of being slightly put out.

"I just received the amended guest list."

She sighed and let the sheets of paper she was holding fall

onto Deirdre as if serving a legal notice.

"You'll see that a number of the guests have certain dietary needs."

Deirdre glanced over some of the names.

"Could you co-ordinate with the caterers please and make sure they're up to speed? When you've taken care of that, go and meet with Security and update them on the list. They should be here soon. Thanks D."

She was gone.

Deirdre knew Security quite well, as Violet tended to hire the same people. Most of them were retired policemen, wearing black. Black was the colour of Security. The white shirt was odd.

†

After four days simmering in his tent, Hugh decided to go home. He set off alone and lightly armed, having refused an escort. By nightfall he had been robbed and taken prisoner. His captors were Eastern Franks, a band of renegade Templars who were widely known to be practitioners of every kind of vice.

They led him for days, tied to the back of an ass, to their remote fortress in the desert. There he was left to languish while they worked out the details of his ransom. Negotiations were drawn-out and came to no satisfactory conclusion, so in the end they decided to cut their losses and sell him into slavery.

†

Sometimes working as a PA for Quag made her feel like an indentured servant. There would be messages at all hours of the day and night with instructions to attend to. It felt like nothing in her life belonged to her. And now this list.

There were vegetarians, carnivores who ate only certain meats, and others who only ate meat cooked in certain ways. People who avoided wheat, or gluten, or unsaturated fats and butter. Fish-eaters and vegans, the lactose intolerant, the herbivores.

Against each name on the list was a dietary preference. The list was long and required some intense discussion with the chef. She wished they could all just eat what they were given. Food did not seem to be the purpose of this event.

That purpose had been shrouded in secrecy from the start. A special group from Security had been loitering in the office during preproduction, gathering documents which had been lying around and shredding them at the end of each day. They also scanned the Internet for relevant images that were tagged with geo-location data. This level of scrutiny was unprecedented. Usually there were only the standard non-disclosure forms to sign. She'd had no idea what it was all about until now. Looking at the names on the list gave her a general sense of the event. It seemed to have something to do with finance.

Sir Neville Dampney – No chicken
Georg Wollenscheidt – Red meat, rare, no sauce
Christine Labide – No red vegetables
Ibn al Kalhoum – Organ meat, no potatoes...

And so on... Two hundred and thirteen names, government finance ministers, or corporate chief financial officers, and their aides. She could not understand what Roger Bellman was doing on the list. He was president of The Egg Board.

†

Three months later, Sir Hugh Berners was sold as a slave to Rashid ad-Din Sinan for a few pieces of gold. Less than what had been hoped for, but better than nothing.

After an arduous journey he was put to work in the kitchens of Masyaf, preparing food for the devotees. It angered him to be a slave of the infidels. As the days went by the anger became a brooding depression and his only relief was to plot his escape. But to leave would be difficult, virtually impossible. He knew he would die there. The cycle of depression continued.

He noticed that one of the men working along side him did not seem to be bothered by his situation. He even appeared to be enjoying his work, taking calm satisfaction in everything he did.

†

When she had finished talking to the head chef, Deirdre went to find Security. They were setting up tables near the side entrance, on the terrazzo-floored mezzanine area above the steps. The employees would have to approach them from below, so they were well placed psychologically and strategically.

Dark blue cloths were being stretched over the tables and neatly clipped at each corner. These tables were the front line for checking in the staff and confiscating their phones or covering the camera lenses with a special security tape, which would indicate tampering. The guests would arrive at the main entrance and would be treated to a more refined process.

A bald man looked her over as she approached. For him, everyone was a suspect with criminal intentions. There was no difference between possibility and actuality. He couldn't help it.

"Hello Kevin."

"Deirdre."

She gave him the list. He had the beginnings of a paunch, tightly contained by his black polo-neck.

"This is the new version."

He took it and thumbed through it, quickly scanning it with his experienced eye. He gave it back.

"We have this already but thanks."

"Tell me something Kevin."

"What's that?"

"Do you have anyone new on your team? I saw someone upstairs. Close cropped blond hair. Slim. About forty. Quite handsome. He had a white shirt on. I think he just threatened me."

Kevin's eyes narrowed.

"No. I don't know anyone like that. What was he doing?"

"I'm not sure. He didn't seem to be doing anything. He told me to go back down. I thought he might be with you."

"And where was this exactly?"

"Come. I'll show you."

†

The man who seemed to gain satisfaction from everything he did, no matter how dull or back-breaking, annoyed Hugh at first but as time passed he became more interesting. Hugh recognized that this man had an approach to life that he would do well to learn.

He had never seen anyone like him before. He was short and slight with skin the colour of hazelnuts. He had a graceful strength and never seemed to tire. He had no beard. While he worked he had the habit of talking to himself in a language that sounded like the buzzing of insects. He laughed frequently. They discovered that they shared a rudimentary knowledge of Latin.

†

The man in the white shirt wasn't there when they went back up the spiral staircase. Kevin looked around. The landing was not very big and had no rooms or closets, so there was not much looking to be done. However he checked underneath the equipment tables, lifting the black fabric which covered them, and found nothing.

"Thanks Deirdre. I'll make a note of this. We'll search the rest of the building. I may bring in some extra people. Tell Quag would you? Probably four more."

The man who was no longer there, was a security agent himself in a way. He belonged to a company called PSS—Parallel Security Services. It wasn't really a company, it just sounded like one. The key word being 'Parallel'. 'Security' was merely a red herring. It was a mercenary organization specializing in covert operations, unaffiliated to any nation, religion, political creed or morality.

The man in the white shirt was in the building to infiltrate its central air conditioning, for tomorrow was to be the first time that *Bathor-9* had been tested outside the laboratory and it had been decided that the ventilation system was the best means of delivery. It would be mixed with vegetable oil and atomized into a fine mist, using carbon dioxide.

†

The beardless man, whose name was Tenpang, said that God was unnecessary. Hugh had never heard anything so ridiculous but the pain of his excommunication made him more receptive.

Suffering was a fruit, grown on a vine and ripened by anger, so it was wrong to kill people, even if they had lived a long time, because there was a ratio between accident and intention, which, if correctly misunderstood, could lead to happiness. Therefore empathy was like the wind. There were nine winds.

Sir Hugh found that he was becoming interested in these ideas, which perhaps were not as outlandish as he had first thought. However these discussions were cut short when he was suddenly removed from his duties in the kitchen.

†

Bathor-9 was a liquid the colour of urine. It was synthesized from the trans-neo clerodane diterpenoid, salvinorin A, naturally found in the plant *Salvia divinorum*, the 'Sage of Ghosts'. Its creators, the brothers and chemists Svenson, had also included their own version of harmaline, a monoamine oxidase inhibitor, a component of the vine *Banisteriopsis caapi*.

This chemical undertaking had been commissioned by PSS, and was believed to be the most powerful hallucinogen known to man. It needed to be tested on the public so that its efficacy as a weapon could be rated. A gathering of the planet's foremost financiers had seemed a suitable place to start.

†

A new target had been chosen. Sir Hugh's Frankish identity would be essential. Though he was not an adherent of the Nizari Ismaili faith, and they considered him an uncultured boor, they were prepared for the first time to make an exception. This is why he was removed from the kitchen. He needed to be trained, and emotionally manipulated, so that he could be trusted to carry out his charge.

Hugh loved to fight. It was his heritage and one of his favourite pastimes. They returned his sword, not the large double-handed one he used from horseback, which he had left in Acre, but the one which had been his father's, and which hung from his belt on a day-to-day basis. He liked that sword, and had not expected to hold it again. It must have been included in his sale. He noticed with approval that it had been cleaned and very well sharpened. He felt like a man again. Fortune was helping him once more. Soon he would swing his arm and harvest some of these heathens. Then he remembered his discussions with Tenpang and thought about his thoughts. It would be wiser to keep his sword sheathed and wait to see what happened.

His training lasted many rigorous months. There was the physical aspect, where he built up his strength and alacrity. A portion of each day was devoted to this activity. Then there was intellectual instruction. This included languages, mathematics, philosophy, astronomy, and alchemy. There was also instruction in comportment. He had to learn how to control his emotions, to remain cold and calculating. Everyday he would be mocked and insulted. Eventually he was able to remain calm under duress. There were classes in invisibility, where he learned how to display or repress the emotions on his face, how to blend and merge, how to use disguise. There was daily instruction in the Nizari Ismaili faith, with much emphasis put on *Ismah*, the infallibility of the prophet and of The Grand Master, who could not commit sin or error because they knew the mind of God. Hugh listened attentively but did not believe. Whether it was because of his excommunication, or his experiences in the Holy Land, he found that he no longer really believed in anything. It came as a surprise, and it bestowed a feeling of liberty that he had not been able to imagine before.

He was aware that he was being prepared to kill someone. He also knew that he had been selected because of who he was. That meant he was expected to act as himself, and that troubled him. If he was to impersonate himself, then who exactly was he?

†

Deirdre had managed to persuade Kevin and Quag to allow her to use the upper landing as her office during the event. She had cleared up the mess of equipment and wires, and had replaced the black tablecloths with white. She didn't mind the long hike to get up and down. She enjoyed it. Her laptop sat on a table alongside a notepad and pen. Security had done a thorough sweep of the building with four additional members and found nothing unusual.

She leaned on the railing and looked down from her vantage point. The guests had all arrived and were milling around the circular tables set out for them, drinks in hand, served by discreet waiters who glided through the crowd with silver trays perched on one flat hand.

Everything was immaculate, starched, and understated. A quiet murmur rose from below. She couldn't help but think of the Titanic. Music was piped in tastefully from somewhere— not too loud, not too soft. All was running smoothly.

Her phone beeped. A text from Quag.

"Can you get down here and make sure the hostesses don't screw up on the seating arrangements?"

The seating arrangements, which had come down from Sir Neville himself, had proven to be a nightmare. They were also the only way the kitchen could get the correct food to each individual. Any error, and disaster would ensue. The guests were not making it easy. Most of them had downed a few glasses by now and they did not wish to be corralled.

Deirdre put her phone in her bag and dashed down the winding staircase. She let one hand brush the outer wall as she went. She felt a girlish excitement. She always did. She knew that Quag was being eaten by anxiety and trying to stay calm. She had probably already taken a pill or two by now.

†

Word came to Sir Hugh that he was ready and that the time was right. He had been assigned a servant, a fellow *fidai* who was to assist him on his mission, cook for him, and do menial work. He was also to use his dagger should Sir Hugh falter. They were not told who they were to assassinate, just where to go. The name would follow.

When they arrived in Ascalon, their target had already gone. He had signed a treaty with Saladin and left by ship. They walked through the remains of the city. Hugh sat down on a rock. It did not matter much to him. He had never intended to carry it out anyway. He pulled his sword from its scabbard and laid it across his knees. He buffed the blade with a cloth. Then he looked up at his servant.

"What now?"

With an unexpected flick of the wrist he slit his servant's throat.

†

About twenty minutes later, all the guests were seated in their correct places. It had not been so difficult. Deirdre made her way back up to her office as Sir Neville Dampney rose from his chair. He was once a handsome man. His cheeks were now veined with thin capillaries but his hair was full and his eyes were still virile. He coughed.

"Ladies and Gentlemen."

Sir Neville had taken an active role in planning this event. He had insisted that there be no dais or podium. Everyone would sit at round tables on the same level. This would foster an atmosphere of democracy but the places had been carefully chosen so that the right people would be talking with each other.

There were at least half a dozen keynote speakers. They were equipped with lavalier wireless microphones in their lapels, which would be turned on by the audio-technician when they rose to speak.

96

Sir Neville continued, "Here today, are gathered the finest minds in the world of finance."

Outside, across the street, hunched in a smart car that was squeezed into a small space, sat a man with a phone held low between his legs. He was watching the proceedings in the bank, fed to him by the surveillance cameras he had placed there. When the guests were settled and Sir Neville Dampney had begun his opening address, he activated the keypad and pressed '9B%$'.

†

Almost three years had passed since Sir Hugh had taken the cross. It was an unpleasant surprise for his wife when he arrived on horseback one sunny morning. Since he had left, she had been in charge along with their eldest son Lambeth, who was fourteen years old. She had first presumed Hugh dead, until she had received the ransom notes, which she ignored. She had been enjoying her new-found power and had no intention of relinquishing it.

Hugh immediately resumed control, as was his right. His first act was to splash cold water on Lambeth's face. He had never taken to that child, who had always been his mother's plaything. Hodierna, his wife, had to resume her place in the marital bed, which was an inconvenience, as she had found another more appealing one.

Further up the chain of command, Sir Hugh's return was also an unwelcome surprise, as it interrupted plans already in motion.

The Regent, who had designs on his lands, despatched the Seneschal with a considerable retinue to visit his part of the country. Hugh was bound by feudal custom to be hospitable. Once arrived, the guests showed no inclination to leave and proceeded to eat him out of business. This prolonged stay gave them time to win over whoever they could. When Hugh realised what was going on he withdrew to the keep.

†

Deirdre had just returned to her office. She sat down with her laptop and perused winter footwear. She looked up from her computer to sip from a glass of water and noticed a pale yellow mist swirling into the room. Sir Neville Dampney was in the middle of his speech, food was being served. Security had noticed it too. There was some frantic movement. The guests were flailing and staggering. The microphones all became live. Disjointed speech filled the room.

As he turned his eyes upward, Sir Neville became seven people, none of whom he knew. Christine Labide had fallen backwards in her chair, mouth frothing.

"... was brilliantly ugly because of the dense sums and Quetzlcoatl..."

She could feel a pressure in her clothes that seemed vegetable in nature. She could not determine colour.

Deirdre could see that Wollenscheidt seemed to be undergoing a paroxysm of ecstasy. She could hear him groaning and sighing as he writhed on the floor, clawing at himself. The mist had risen in the room and was drifting towards her. She jumped back, spilling the glass of water.

Then she became a man.

†

He can hear the clanking of steel. People are coming up. Heart pounding, he rips the sword from its sheath. The first man is upon him, struggling to find the space to swing. He cuts him down. Then the second. Black bearded, slipping in blood. He shoves his sword with both hands into the rib cage. Fear and delight. He uses his foot to help free his weapon and to push the man back down onto his comrades below him. The next one comes up from the gloom, then the next, then one more. This one is swinging widely.

"Shit. He's left-handed..."

Five Minutes

"Do you have five minutes?"

"No. Not really. What do you want?"

These were unspoken thoughts. People need time and attention but there is a limited amount of time, so you have to be judicious.

I wondered why this stranger was accosting me. He looked a bit like Harry Death, a momentary peripheral figure from my childhood, red-bearded and garbed in black clothes from another era. Rumours swirled about Harry. He slept in a coffin surrounded by skulls and candles with dripping wax. The man at the centre of all this was an enigma, neither confirming nor denying, never speaking. Here they differed because this man before me wanted to talk.

"Do you have five minutes?"

The best thing was not to answer.

"Why?"

"If you give me five minutes, I'll tell you my life."

There was a lot that could be done with time. It could be spent as a currency. It could be presented as a gift, or wasted as a valuable commodity. It could swirl down the drain like water, owned by everyone and by no one. But the idea of a life recounted in five minutes was interesting. This was the kind of memoir that appealed to me.

"Okay then. Tell me."

He did not start talking right away. A hint of doubt crossed his face as if he was surprised that I had agreed to listen, or whether he would be able to deliver on his offer. He cleared his throat and rapidly began to speak in bursts of clipped sentences.

"Born into the post-war. Ration books just gone, meagre fare, gaps in the buildings, hand-me-down clothes. I'm wearing the plastic helmet which I've cut into the shape of a German one. I'm holding my Sten gun which must serve as a Schmeiser. I've got my sister and her friend up against the wall outside the house and I demand that they show me their papers. They are older and humour me. At night the lamppost on the corner bathes the ground in amber light. It is very quiet. Up at the end of the street is the alley where someone was killed once and thrown over a wall.

My best friend lives halfway up the road. In the summer we get to each other's houses by climbing along the walls in people's back gardens. No one seems to mind. Sometimes we creep up behind the milk float and try to steal bottles of milk. The milkman always sees us in the mirror and slams on the brakes. We get bruised shins and no milk.

My father opens his white shirt and manages to clear almost everything from the table into it. Maybe he's had too much to drink but his appreciation of the absurd, so often buried in remote parts of his character has stayed with me forever. Who is this man? He brings me postcards of Magritte paintings when he comes home from work. I am the youngest.

I have been sent to my room because I hit my brother. Now I can come out, except I won't. I've managed to lock the door. All manner of pleading and bribery won't move me. If I open the door I can go and change the gears on the Land Rover which belongs to someone who is visiting. I will not. There is a ladder. They are coming up over the roof.

All kinds of interesting things can be found in the cupboard under the stairs which smells of floor polish. There are things from the war, ominous and pristine.

Then it's off to school one day. Dropped off on the gravel driveway of an old manor house with leaded windows. I've got a uniform with my name sewn into it and a box my father made with my number on it—sixty-four. There's some sniffling and home-sickness among the seven year-olds. We have toughening up practice every morning in the dormitory when we wake up. An older boy lines us new boys up. He walks down the line, randomly hitting people in the face. You must not cry.

Mrs. Gibbs teaches the young boys math. She invites us into her garden full of lovely flowers with chickens wandering around and peacocks. She gives us tea and scones. She shows us the wild pond teeming with insect life. She reads us stories. Mr. Gibbs doesn't seem to exist.

But when we get a little older they take Mrs. Gibbs away from us. Now it is to be boxing, Latin and football. No more women. The only woman we'll have dealings with now, is the matron, and only when we are ill or injured.

It is a pleasure to come down with something contagious and be confined to the sick-room. We don't have to do any lessons, just lie in bed and read all day. The matron brings food and she is nice to us. The windows of the sickroom open over the place where the teachers and headmaster park their cars. At night we stand on the sill and piss out of the window. The sound of our urine hitting the metal roofs of the cars below fills us with laughter.

Until we are eleven we wear shorts. We get chapped skin and chilblains in the winter from walking through the snow. Our thighs get red and sore and hurt a lot under hot water. In the summer we swim naked. When we climb out of the pool we run around whipping each other with our towels, the smell of cut grass is in the air. We like to throw marbles into this grass. They damage the mowers which manicure the cricket pitch. There is always an enquiry to find the culprit. If no one owns up there will be group punishment. Even the innocent will suffer. It makes me think of the Germans. But no one confesses and no one snitches.

All the food we are given must be eaten, down to the last morsel. It is not important if we like it or not. This rule is enforced. Every boy has to do clean-up duty in the dining room after meals. That means we have to clean up the teachers' plates too. They eat with us but sit at a table on a dais at one end of the room. Their food is much better than ours, so one of the perks of clean-up duty is eating the scraps the masters have left on their plates. In the afternoons we get a slice of bread with yellow butter and a small bottle of milk. I think the government provides the milk.

Everyday in the morning we must take a shit. Afterwards we must put a tick in the box next to our names. Failure to do so will cause us to be publicly questioned and hauled off to the doctor.

Wednesday afternoons are free of compulsory sport and we can play in the woods with minimal supervision. A master is on patrol but this is our world and we know it much better than he does. We hide when he approaches. After he has passed us we can resume exploring and tree-climbing. We dam the stream, walking in it with Wellington boots. Sometimes it sloshes over the tops and makes for wet feet. We build secret defensive structures and form gangs, fighting over territory.

The woods are a long sliver of wilderness flanking the playing field. They are bordered on the other side by the stream. There are three distinct zones. At one end there is a huge and dense bamboo thicket, with thick stems towering up twenty feet. This is an area through which we make a labyrinth of tunnels. The other end is a pine forest, mysterious and brown, dead needles on the ground. A strangely still and silent place with an air of foreboding. The middle zone is lush with leaves. There is a fallen tree which rests in the fork of another. The climb is a little dangerous but is rewarded with a crow's nest of foliage which we augment with branches to make a perfect vantage point. This fallen tree is worth fighting for. Occasionally the younger boys are hunted and beaten with bamboos when caught.

Once every couple of months is the hair harvest. This is when the barber comes to visit. He sets himself up in the bathroom and no one escapes his chair. Short back and sides for all. We are frightened of the barber.

T'was snippig and the greasy clip
did hum and mumble for the tress.
All flimsy were the locks that nip
and barber cause the prey distress.

That's what Julian Roberts said about it.

On a limited number of Sundays we are allowed to be visited by our parents and taken out for the day. Sometimes my father comes, and sometimes my mother. Never together. My mother usually arrives late in her Lancia. I am waiting alone at the door as all the other boys have left. Eventually she arrives and we drive off somewhere. I'm sure my parents were wondering what they could do with their estranged son for six hours after the drive down from London. We might go for a walk, or visit an old site, the day culminating in a damp hotel dining room having a cream tea. When she drops me back at school I have to fight off the surge of rekindled sadness and resume my customary indifference to homesickness.

On other occasions I am invited to go out with a friend and his parents. We cram into their old Dormobile with the dogs, and drive off to the New Forest for a picnic. This forest is not new anymore. It was once—almost nine hundred years ago when William Rufus claimed it for his personal hunting ground, displacing any peasants who happened to be there. And it was there that his body was found after a so-called hunting accident and hauled out on a cart.

1066 to 1087, 1087 to 1100, 1100 to 1135, 1135 to 1154, 1154 to 1189, 1189 to 1199, 1199 to 1216. Get the dates and the monarchs wrong and Captain Hill, of the gammy leg, will slap your buttocks and let his hand rest there a while, as you stand next to him trying to amuse yourself and the class by pulling out the thin strands of his hair that are brushed across his almost bald pate. He chain smokes and throws the butts out of the upper window behind him without looking. We like to close that window and laugh as the cigarette ends fall harmlessly to the sill and he never seems to notice.

The New Forest is one of two magical forests that I know. The other is the Forest of Dean. I have wandered in both. But it is in the New Forest that I discover a predilection for deliberately getting lost and then finding my way back. Call it problem solving."

"Hold on."

"What?"

He looked at me quizzically as he came down from the detached intensity of his monologue.

"This is all very interesting but you've been talking for more than five minutes."

"I have? But I haven't finished yet. I don't want to leave you with the wrong impression."

"You said you could tell me your life in five minutes. That's what we agreed on."

"Don't you have a little more time?"

"No. I'm sorry but I have to go. Thanks for your story."

He looked worried.

"Listen. One minute. If I paid you six hundred pounds, would you kill me? You could make it look like an accident."

"No thanks, I can't help you there."

An English Story

In a land of reclaimed rivers, pulverized minerals and wheeler-dealers, were three men who formed a psycho-anarchic syndicate. They all desired the same woman.

The three of them made a vast inverted triangle over southern England, with Sydney Gristmill occupying the apex in Bridport, Dorset, not far from Portland Castle. Sydney Gristmill had a severe madarosis, which left neither hair on his brow nor lash on his lid. This condition unnerved the objects of his steady gaze and tended to squelch friendships before they had the chance to ignite. He was lonely.

Polder was further out west in Taunton. It was a far cry from the child he had been, to the man he had become. Something had happened along the way, too serious to talk about. It had caused an unusually high level of dampness, resulting in melancholia. Not an attractive prospect for females.

George Chapman moved around a lot, but Inland Revenue had an address for him in Guildford. He was a friendly man with lips poised to smile, and whose smiles always verged on laughter. His good humour was accompanied by a fondness for food and drink which left him abdominous in physique. George Chapman was also pathologically dishonest. He was simply unable to tell the truth. He didn't even know what it was.

One night, under a decrescent moon, these three points converged in a public house in West London. It was just after nine and The Crumb and Horse was doing a brisk trade. Lancer had his head on the table next to his unfinished pint of ESB. He was an old soldier, and a regular since before anyone else present had been born. It was only at closing time, when he didn't get up, that he was discovered to be dead. Until that moment they respectfully let him sleep, besides, he always nursed his pint.

Michael Polder stood at the bar, eyeing the woman behind it. He was searching for something to say but she never gave him the opportunity. Whenever she was nearby, her attention was engaged by something else—anything but him. Then she would move away again quickly. He watched silently as Chapman, who was at the other end, made her laugh every time she passed. Gristmill sat alone at a table by the door, glaring at anybody who noticed him. These three men had never met. Their syndicate was an unconscious one, more to do with the linkage of events than any individual cognition.

The clock on the wall marked the inexorable approach of closing time. It was a cycle, this opening and closing, akin to the waxing and waning of a moon or the beating of a heart. Coupled with the ancient history of the hop, the mystery was complete. With handshakes and micturition the clientele thinned, and the men made their way home to their lonely wives. One of them accidentally shat himself upon a cough.

Polder and Chapman had moved closer together at the bar. Now that she was markedly less busy, the barmaid knew that some kind of conversation was going to become inevitable. The one with the face like a skull had been trying to talk to her all night. He was persistent. She had taken some pleasure in pretending not to notice him. Unsolicited attention was part of the job. Most of it was from drunken men, and ran the gamut between muddled sincerity and outright leering. She had strategies to deal with most situations, so well-worn they didn't require thought. The last, and most tangible, was the cricket bat beneath the bar, which she had never needed to use. One of her roles at The Crumb and Horse was matriarchal, dispensing sympathy and medicine in equal measures, and chiding where necessary. She also played the elusive maiden, fleeting through the imaginations of her customers. Behind it all was her own life, her own man and child. None of the patrons could conceive of that, except the women perhaps, and they were few. Thirty five minutes to go and she would be free. It was the man by the door who disturbed her most, ogling her with his strange eyes. He looked the type to follow her home.

"Last orders gentlemen."

She would address them both. It was simpler that way. They wanted refills.

"I haven't seen you here before. Where are you from?"

The skull opened his mouth but the fat one cut him off.

"You don't remember me? I live around the corner. I'm in here all the time."

She doubted herself briefly.

"Surely you recognize my friend?"

After a fractional delay she realised that the friend he was referring to was his belly, which he rubbed with a big hand, eyes a'twinkle. She wasn't sure what to make of it.

Chance, tempered by fate had brought Chapman, Polder and Gristmill to The Crumb and Horse that evening. A visit, scheduled the next morning, to a specialist at Hammersmith Hospital regarding his hair loss, was causing Gristmill anxiety and was dragging down his mood, which was never above average anyway. He had reserved a room on Rylett Road. Chapman was in the area to broker a deal with a local felon, on a large number of cigarettes he had come by. Michael Polder was in West London to attend an afternoon of poetry readings. All of their plans hinged on the following day. They could have gone to any pub but they all ended up at 'The Horse'. Perhaps it was the unusual sign that had attracted them, prehistoric and schematic, like the horse on the Berkshire Downs. Once inside, they came to desire the barmaid.

Now, including Lancer who was still asleep, there were only five of them left in the place. It was becoming too intimate. She was thinking she would lock up, let them finish their pints and send them on their way.

Chapman had his forearms on the bar. He was trying to peer over it surreptitiously, without her noticing. She had an interesting way of moving—nothing was wasted, each hand on a separate task. Her straight black hair was tied up behind, and her eyes, done up like Nefertiti, would slip through his gaze as he tried to catch them.

"What's your name then?"

Before she had time to answer, two men burst through the door. They might have been brothers, both large, ruddy and middle aged, still living the life of the fist. Everything about them was hasty, which seemed incongruous for such big men. The door had not even swung shut when one of them yelled.

"Stand back from the bar lads."

Within seconds chairs and tables were flying and glass was breaking. She ducked down low next to the cricket bat. Chapman had taken off to the back room, where the dartboard was. Gristmill and Lancer remained at their tables. Polder stayed at the bar, bemused by the rapidity of events, and unable to register danger. They paid him no attention. Then the men were gone, as suddenly as they had arrived.

The barmaid stood up and took in the damage. Every single bottle and glass on the back bar was smashed.

"Looks like Mathers missed a payment. Everyone alright?"

She saw that Polder was racked with emotion and seemed as if he was about to cry.

"Come on. You can all have another for your troubles. Draught only I'm afraid."

Chapman was back. She glanced over at Gristmill.

"You want one, love?"

"I'll take a London Pride."

She poured the drinks, and walked over to Lancer, gently tapping him on the shoulder.

"Time to go home, dear."

When he didn't stir, she tapped him again, a little harder. Then she felt his neck and lifted his head with both hands.

"My God he's dead. The old bugger."

She put his head back on the table, paced a circle momentarily, then opened the door and stepped out. When she came back in, Chapman, Polder and Gristmill glimpsed a woman they hadn't noticed before. Decisive, cool under stress, authoritative.

"You're going to have to help me out boys. There's a telephone box a few yards up the street. Take old Lancer here, and put him in it."

She felt their hesitation.

"He died of natural causes. He was an old man. It doesn't make any difference if he died here or in a phone box. We just don't want the law coming round asking questions, do we? We're not doing anything wrong."

They could see her point.

She kept lookout as they struggled to get Lancer out of his chair. The meaning of deadweight became apparent. Gristmill was taking most of the burden. As they left the building, Chapman was grinning.

"What a way to go. Fuck me. It couldn't get much better than that. Well, unless…"

He looked over his shoulder at her as they stumbled past. The street outside was quiet. Anyway, there was nothing unusual about a man being helped home by his mates when he was a little the worse for wear. She watched as they propped Lancer up in the telephone box and then she locked the door.

Though she found each one of them unattractive, their individual qualities of humour, sensitivity and strength, when taken together, would make a tolerable human being.

Yellow Pendragon

Clive Bond drove a back hoe for the highway department. As a child he had spent muddy afternoons carving out trenches in clay-laden soil and filling them with water. Now he dug holes in roads.

As his hands operated the levers, his mind escaped the dirty, cramped confines of his spartan cab. It was on such a flight of fancy that he had once considered the nature of causes, and returned unsure whether they could be said to exist.

Though he didn't know it, he had come closer then, with those thoughts, to approximating his position in the scheme of things. He had come close once before when he blamed the depression to which he was occasionally subject on a cave-dwelling ancestor some thirty thousand years earlier. It was a depressing idea in itself to realise that one was locked into a genetic prison and there was really nothing that could be done. It came as a relief when he learned that such genetic inheritance did not generally transcend twenty-eight generations.

Whenever he turned off the motor, he would sit back on his seat and enjoy the sudden lack of noise. It came as a burst of silence, thick and syrupy. Then within moments its hyper-reality would subside, leaving him to wonder where the silence had gone. He would become more conscious of the outside world and hear perhaps a cackling in the sky. He might look up and see a flock of geese high above him, making their way south for the winter.

Clive did not know that each hole he dug was bringing him ever closer to a sinkhole—a hole where meaning was going to get out of hand. And he had never heard of Samantha Ray.

Samantha had been dead almost a hundred years when Clive

was born, but had she still been alive they would have been separated by only a few miles.

She was a farm girl and did what farm girls did—milked cows, churned butter, assisted with the delivery of calves and the castration of rams. But Samantha Ray was unable to conform to the expectations people held for women in those days and was a source of disappointment to her family. She was still unmarried and had no prospects.

Somehow she managed to find the time to wander alone in the countryside. She saw herself as Joan of Arc. She didn't know much about Joan but liked what she knew. At night she kept her sister awake with the incessant murmuring of her prayers.

Samantha never spoke of her country rambles. But one evening she did not return home as expected. Her family were worried and planned to go and search for her but then she reappeared mud-spattered and bedraggled.

This time she spoke of her experience, perhaps because the ire of her father demanded it, or because what she had discovered needed to be heard. She had received knowledge from a robed and bearded man. It had been raining and she had taken shelter in a hollow beneath an overhang. She was waiting for the rain to stop before finding her way home. It was getting dark and she was beginning to feel apprehensive when she had suddenly realised she was not alone. An old man sat on the other side of the hollow with his knees drawn up to his chest and his arms tightly wrapped around him. He was mumbling softly. She understood he was talking to her. He spoke in a strange accent.

"Do you know who I am, girl?"

"No, Sir."

"No matter, but I am old. Older than you can imagine. I will die tonight. Listen carefully and remember what I tell you."

The old man clenched himself against the cold.

"There is a sleeping king not far from here in a cave. He is suspended in a magical slumber where life and death are one. When the need for him is great enough he will rise and do battle to ensure peace and happiness for all people."

Samantha listened with rapt attention and forgot about her fear of walking through the woods in the dark. Could this old man be talking about the return of The Saviour?

"Why are you telling me this?"

"I have been many things to King Arthur—his guardian, his mentor, his counsel. Because of this I have been awake for years. I cannot join him in his enchanted sleep, as I am bound to the laws of mortality, though I have been able to cheat them for some time. If my knowledge dies with me, then he will never wake up. The world will become an abyss. So now I have told you, and you are his standard bearer. Never shirk this responsibility."

She speculated that she had been chosen by God to announce his return. It seemed a fitting reward for her lonely life. But she needed something—a confirmation that she had been selected by the Almighty.

"Why have you chosen me?"

"Because you are here. There is no one else."

Perhaps it was her vanity, she thought, that made her need to feel chosen. Though it was possible that God had guided her steps to this man, or angel—for he must be an angel. Everyone knew that God acted mysteriously.

Clive sensed the day was going to go badly when he set off for work at 5:00am. As he was getting into his car, he discovered that the unicorn was no longer in his pocket. He had found it at the side of the road. It was white and plastic, probably a lost or discarded toy. At the time, he realised that he had never seen a toy unicorn before, so he picked it up and put it into the pocket of his work jacket where it had remained ever since. But now it had gone.

He didn't consider himself superstitious, but the unicorn's disappearance was so out of the ordinary that it made him feel uneasy. He probably should have gone back inside to look for it but made a snap decision to keep going. He had two jobs that day—his normal one, and something that he had taken on the side—excavating an old sceptic tank. So he shrugged to himself and set off. That was his first mistake.

Mist hung low in the pre-dawn and visibility was bad. He noticed thousands of disembodied eyes on each side of the road, glowing through the fog. There were a lot of animals in the world but this seemed an unnaturally large number to congregate in one place. He was looking out at the eyes all around him when he suddenly felt a sickening bump. He knew he had just killed something small—probably a groundhog or a squirrel.

"Shit!"

He hated that aspect of humanity which caused it to kill things, often without any awareness at all. Every step taken meant death for something else.

As he recoiled inwardly from what he had just done, he saw the form of a ghostly stag leap through the beam of his head-lights, antlers silhouetted against the creeping dawn.

He tried to react but there was not enough time. The impact was considerable, and not just a sickening bump. He stopped abruptly, got out and walked around to the front of the vehicle expecting to see the mangled corpse of the stag, or even worse that it would still be alive and writhing in pain. Then he would have to kill it himself. Nausea welled up with dull persistence. But the animal had gone. There was no sign of him except for a dent in the front quarter panel on the driver's side. At least he was alive.

He got back into his car and drove the remaining mile to the lot where he kept his back hoe. He had chained it up on a flatbed the night before. He drove the rest of the way to Church Street slowly and in a state of numb alertness.

The home owner was waiting for him on the porch—Rex Ray. With a name like that he could be a character in a Batman film. The Rays were an old family. They had been in the area for hundreds of years. The hard work of their forbears had slowly born fruit, for now the many family members were all landowners and most of them were quite well-off.

He didn't really like the Rays, not that he knew any of them personally. It was more a dislike on principal, or a prejudice. Those old families seemed clannish and inbred. Everyone else was a newcomer to them, an outsider, a boat-person. No doubt they harboured centuries of tangled secrets, bodies buried in the woods. They were supercilious in a sly, uneducated way.

Clive had received an extensive education himself, though he had chosen not to make use of it. He had dispensed with the title "Dr." that he could have put before his name. After all, Wittgenstein had worked with his hands, turning his back on philosophy. The higher value given in society to mental, as opposed to manual labour chafed on Clive. It seemed to him an ancient capitalist conspiracy which conveniently forgot that manual labour also required mental work. What if all the working people just walked away, like the servants of Czar Nicholas who abandoned him and left him alone to his fate in his empty palace?

Rex Ray looked impatient as he jumped down from the cab. It wasn't even six o'clock. Clive was in a bad mood.

"Are you Bond?"

"Bond, yes. But you can call me Clive."

"Well let's get on with it."

"That's why I'm here."

He strode back to the truck, tilted the bed and unchained the machine. He looked around the site.

"You didn't put any markers up like we agreed."

There was an overpowering smell of shit in the air. The tank should have been pulled years ago. He was probably too cheap and had held off till the last minute.

"I know exactly where it is. I'll show you."

"Are there any underground electric cables I should be aware of?"

"No."

Rex Ray wondered if this man was up for the job. He'd come recommended but he seemed angry. Still, time was running out and he didn't have any other options. He had spent years researching, investigating and looking. Now he was confident he had located the cave where Arthur and his companions were sleeping. Unfortunately it was beneath the sceptic tank.

He knew that the tank was old and that a replacement was long overdue. His search for Arthur's resting place had been exhaustive. At the same time he had been trying to create a system that measured the severity of crises. He had always wanted to know when the sleeping king would wake up. This had meant a lot of work in order to amass the requisite figures and statistics—levels of poverty, civil unrest, median incomes, job opportunities, nutrition, warfare, education, public health, life expectancy and so on. This, in conjunction with his search for the cave had left him little time for anything else.

Ever since childhood he had felt a strong affinity to his great aunt Samantha. She had been maligned, treated with indifference, ignored and regarded as unbalanced but he believed her. He knew that he was her representative, and he knew how important it was. It didn't matter what other people thought.

He also knew that crisis, in the country and in the world at large had reached a dangerous threshold. One might have thought that the turmoil of the mid twentieth century would have rung the alarm clock. But the situation now was even more complex. It was no longer just about the deranged visions of demagogues, though they were not in short supply. The king was about to wake up—anytime now, but his egress would be blocked by the sceptic tank and that would ring a death-knell for humanity.

Mr. Bond had started to scrape away the surface. It made Rex Ray uneasy to watch such a coarse machine attempt such a sensitive task.

"Be careful."

"Asshole" thought Clive as his nimble hands dropped the great shovel. The clank and clatter, and the sounds of the motor and relentless motion made their muffled way to the cavern below. Arthur Pendragon opened his eyes. He might as well have kept them shut as it was pitch dark and he couldn't see a thing. He instinctively groped around for his sword before remembering that he had thrown it in a lake somewhere. A stupid lack of forethought. Still, he would take one from one of his men. But where were they? He would find the way out, then go back for them. There ought to be a chink of light. He had been asleep so long he felt sluggish. His memory was hazy and dreamlike but he seemed to remember that the cave they had entered was not too deep. There should be an opening nearby but there didn't seem to be one.

He felt his way along the wall with his hands. There was not much air in this place, and what little remained was fetid and stank of shit. He was going to have to get out soon, or he never would. He could hear noises above him. It sounded like a battle. Things must be bad. But at least it meant that he was not too far from the surface.

He felt earth falling on his face, then a rumbling started and the chamber opened up, letting in a gust of air. For a second he saw daylight shining in, then a huge yellow dragon was falling down on him.

"You fucking idiot. Do you know what you've done?"

Clive had banged his head when the back hoe tipped forward. Blood was gushing from his forehead and obscured his vision. Rex Ray seemed to be shouting at him. He managed to shut off the engine and wipe the blood from his eyes. A gale force wind had whipped up out of nowhere. Rex Ray was standing on the rim of the crater, frenzied and gesticulating. The sky behind him, which had been getting lighter before was now darkening at an alarming rate.

He had never seen anything like this before. His limbs froze but his mind was frantically searching for a way out. He watched as Mr. Ray tumbled into the pit like a discarded puppet. And now, as he hung suspended in his machine, the horrible realisation came to him…

Inside the Greenhouse

Sir Cecil Hobbes returned to England early in 1857, just before the Sepoy Mutiny. He had worked for John Company his entire adult life and England seemed like a foreign country to him. Still, he came back wealthier than many princes and even had the audacity to buy himself a seat in Parliament. At heart he was not a parliamentarian and he slept through the few sessions he attended, instructing an aide to wake him if anything important occurred. Eventually he ceased to attend altogether. He bought fifty acres in Oxfordshire and had a fine house built.

Sir Cecil was a man of varied interests, and with the means to pursue them. A curiosity about the flora of the tropical zone caused him to have a lavish greenhouse of glass and wrought iron built alongside his house. The interior, heated and humidified, quickly became a jungle. He was also an amateur lepidopterist and a writer of nonsense verse. It is said that he smoked one pipe of opium before bed every night for the last forty years of his life.

Aside from his servants, he lived alone and died without heirs.

The house passed through a succession of owners, the penultimate being Chas. Rearden, who made his money on the black market during the Second World War. He only occupied it briefly before he died from an aneurism. He was discovered face down in the greenhouse by his driver who noticed a butterfly tattooed on the back of his neck that he hadn't seen before. Mr. Rearden had bequeathed the house to the Catholic Church—perhaps in a last ditch attempt to seek indulgence for his questionable life. He was never known to be religious. It was used as a retreat for nuns until it burned down in 1958.

The Church sold the greenhouse and a few acres to my father. The rest of the estate was divided and sold off as parcels to developers.

The greenhouse is where I now live, or more exactly, I live in a tent inside a house, inside the greenhouse. It is no longer tropical.

I'm not sure when I first became fascinated by structures within structures. It might have been a visit to the temple of Dendur in the Metropolitan Museum of Art in New York, or it might have started earlier as an amorphous idea that was given shape by the temple—a reconstructed building that was housed inside another building which in some way resembled a very grand greenhouse.

I went back to see it again some years later and was denied access. That whole wing of the museum had been rented out for a private party and was cordoned off. I was annoyed that a space intended for the benefit of the public had been usurped by a few wealthy people. That was the arrogance of money. I wanted none of it—the arrogance that is. In hindsight I've come to think that these few rich people confirmed my own desires. Why hold a party in such a place if not for the allure of a building within a building? Of course they may have just been milling about, attracted by the setting which was pleasing to the eye, without sharing my particular affinity.

Since that visit to the museum the idea had never been far from my mind—mostly forgotten but quick to resurface under the right stimulus. A subconscious desire. I wondered about its underlying psychology. A house provided both real and symbolic protection. What kind of person would want to put a house inside a house? Someone who felt more threatened than most? Did the double layer give added protection to the person, or to the building that sheltered the person? Was there any real difference?

I imagined there would be a variety of ecological environments within the containing structure—sandy areas, a stream, grassland in miniature, or moss. There would also be an internal

120

weather system that would control itself and I would sometimes have to deal with a downpour or gusty winds. It seemed as if I was trying to bring the outdoors inside. The psychology of protection from threat came up short. It didn't address the aesthetics of my personal biosphere. It wasn't fear alone that inspired this architectural fantasy.

When I inherited the greenhouse, idea became substance. Aside from being the new owner, other aspects of my life were perfectly aligned—my marriages had run their course, my children were adult and busy elsewhere with their own lives. I had the idea that the twilight years of my life, of which I was becoming increasingly aware, should be spent in contemplation.

Possibly Sir Cecil had felt the same way, turning his back on public life and composing doggerel in his leafy shrine. It was a concept he might have picked up in India, where I've heard it is not uncommon for an ageing patriarch, having fulfilled years of familial duty, to retreat into meditation. A preparation for the grave perhaps, or the pyre. Pondering these means of disposal made me think about a body being laid out in the open, dealt with by the elements and scavengers, the bones being collected at a later date and buried beneath a cairn. I am convinced this practice is called 'excarnation', though I have not been able to find the word in any dictionary.

But the Indian patriarch would not have been able to lead such an existence, were it not for the women who cared for him. Their unquestioned, unnoticed subjugation made even the noblest ideas seem stupid and mean.

My case was different. I looked after myself, aided by the dwindling supply of money which still remained from the fortune of my forbears. I was not looking for a life of total seclusion but I too was tired of duty.

With Dendur in mind, I built a box-like house from concrete blocks. I stuccoed the walls inside and out with plaster, tinted with raw umber and burnt sienna. After I had sanded the walls smooth, I sealed them with varnish. The roof was wooden and flat, with extended joists. The structure was off-centred in the greenhouse because that position was the most pleasing to me.

Sir Cecil's tropical plants had disappeared long before my arrival, but I cultivated weeds and grasses, or allowed them to cultivate themselves. I had several truck loads of sand delivered and spread it over one end of the greenhouse. I spent time and effort sculpting it into dunes which reminded me of the Canary Islands. But the gap between intention and execution can be quite wide. I never made a stream or an autonomous weather system. After an initial burst of effort which lasted about three years, I settled into an acceptance of my greenhouse for the way it was and made no further attempt to change it.

I happily lived a life of minimal subsistence. I spent money only on essential requirements, and those I whittled to the bone. It was not out of miserliness that I lived this way but from a natural aversion to consumption.

And then the phone started ringing. But I didn't have a phone. It began with the butterflies. I didn't think much of them at first, other than being impressed by their beauty. In retrospect it was odd because I had never seen butterflies in the greenhouse before, until one day they appeared in large numbers. Not long after that the non-existent telephone started to ring.

Even though I knew I did not have a phone I looked everywhere just to be certain. When I didn't find one I went to a doctor, thinking I might be suffering from tinnitus but the doctor could find nothing wrong with my hearing. She said I was anaemic and prescribed one pint of Guinness to be drank per day. Brain scans and X-rays provided no explanation for my auditory hallucinations. So in the end I went home knowing I would have to live with an occasional but interminably ringing telephone.

Every time it rang my stress level was raised. There was a malevolence to the sound. I felt as if someone was watching me. I was also interrupted by the weather which had found its way in. Vandals had broken several panes with stones. Most likely they were teenagers exercising their predatory instincts in an act of frustration and impotence.

I was unable to summon the motivation to repair the damage and, as with the ringing telephone, learned to live with it. Perhaps it was an aspect of ageing that the bar seemed to be constantly lowered in regard to what was acceptable. I set up a tent in the temple and life went on.

I wondered if the place was haunted and Sir Cecil was expressing his resentment towards me for inhabiting his greenhouse. But I didn't believe in ghosts. Still... Some things may never be explained.

I began to spend more time in the tent writing verse, interrupted by the telephone. And then the tiger was delivered.

Deliveries were rare occurrences. This was particularly strange as I had not ordered anything. A large van pulled up outside and the driver sounded his horn impatiently. He made me sign his electronic pad, and with the help of his assistant heaved a large crate on to the ground. Then the van disappeared in a cloud of dust. I pried open the crate to discover a replica of Tipu's Tiger. It was almost six feet long and about two feet high. This replica was made from hard plastic instead of wood, and the mechanism was not powered by a hand crank like the original but by batteries which were included. Despite being made from plastic, it was a good likeness, right down to the tiger's testicles. I had seen the original in the Victoria and Albert museum. This automaton, so much a piece of the 18th century when the word 'robot' had not yet been invented, was also a musical instrument. I checked the side and sure enough, hidden away beneath a small cover was a keyboard. In the fascination of the moment I forgot to think about who might have sent this to me. That would come later. I inserted the batteries, found the switch and turned it on.

The red-coated, black-hatted European pinned beneath the tiger, began to flail his left arm. This victim was often referred to as European but it seemed obvious to me that he was English—an employee of John Company and probably a soldier in one of its private armies. The tiger roared repeatedly and the moving arm kept rising and falling back down to the victim's mouth as he shrieked. This produced a strange ululation that reminded me of the sounds I had made as a child when playing Cowboys and Indians with my friends.

Though I had never seen the original automaton functioning, I had read about it. This new replica differed in the means of its sound production. It used samples of real screams and roars as opposed to generating them with bellows, though the result, emitted through a small cheap speaker was no closer to reality. That was when I began to wonder about the reason for this unrequested delivery. It might have been a coded message.

Tipu Sultan was the king of Mysore and an implacable foe of the British. With his rocketry and his French-trained army, he had won several battles against the soldiers of John Company. He had a tiger throne. The tiger was his totem. Perhaps this automaton was more than just a sadistic entertainment for him. It might have been a weapon on the mythical plane, where a representation of his victory over the English would make it happen in the fleshy world. He might as well have ordered the sea to recede, for his victories were pyrrhic and he was swept away in an ocean of European history. He was killed in his palace at the culmination of a siege and his kingdom was absorbed by John Company.

Why the piece was also a musical instrument perplexed me, unless the keyboard existed to accompany rituals. Perhaps the vibration of musical notes augmented the efficacy of the sculpted image in some Pythagorean way.

This haunting, whether by ghosts, malicious strangers, or even by my own mind drove me further into seclusion. I began to understand what Sir Cecil Hobbes had been doing in his old age.

As hopes and aspirations flaked away and opinions once held so strongly became unconvincing, nonsense verse was the purest expression of reality.

With that realisation came the understanding that reality was something to be expressed and not just experienced.

A field of grass was fast enough
To soon become a meadow,
Through which a botanizer passed
With purple in his shadow.

I shouted at him from afar.
I beckoned him with onions.
I offered pheasants in a jar
With serpents twined among them.

"Enough, enough, enough," he cried
And struck me with a feather.
He asked me if I was the son
Of Captain Merriweather.

The light that glanced across his eye
Was straighter than two arrows.
First it set my hat ablaze then
Frightened off the sparrows.

The botanizer raised his arm
And dropped it to his side,
Then flung himself upon the ground
And cursed the swollen tide.

"If yesterday" the old man said.
"Came close behind tomorrow,
Where would I find my tiger's head?"
He wept salt tears of sorrow.

"Dad? Dad? Can you hear me?... It's me, Julie. My God you look terrible. It's a good thing we came here. We're going to take you back with us and look after you for a bit. Ben? Can you come here and help me pick him up? You look like you could do with some food. Why are there so many butterflies everywhere?"

125

The Promoter

"I'm a promoter."

"Of musicians?"

"No. I try to stay away from musicians."

"A promoter of yourself then?" I asked.

Anton shrugged and smiled.

"It's hard to completely divorce the self from its surroundings."

That was my first conversation with him. It was in a coffee shop. He was attaching something to the wall.

Anton did not stay in town for long—three months at most. People assumed he had come from the city but no one knew for sure. That was one of the strange things about Anton, the more you thought about him, the less you knew.

In the short time he was here, he acquainted himself with just about everyone in town and could greet each one by name. He was full of social grace and could talk to people easily. I understood later he had a method. He would coax people to talk about themselves, which is what most people want to do anyway. This gave the impression of a deep and harmonious exchange that would not appear one-sided until later. By then he would be gone.

Anton had the ability to turn things inside out. Though he gave little of himself away, he managed to use peoples' rambling self-explications as a vehicle to give them back one single idea. It was never more than one per conversation.

I learned from talking about myself numerous times that the Möbius Strip is the geometrical expression of truth and beauty. Tourism eats culture from the inside. Gentrification is akin to modern global agriculture. Both of them stifle variety. People should pile stones one on top of the other. They will one day learn to build cities. Time is a solid object that behaves like a liquid. Failure is an asset. Absurdity is an unguent.

Falsehood and truth were irrelevant in Anton. I pushed him once for details of his past and he curtly informed me that he was older than both of his parents. I had a friend who was enamoured of him. She told me that he always managed to deflect her advances. Eventually, when she realized she was getting nowhere, she asked him if he found her ugly. He looked at her with his sweet smile and said that he found her both ugly and extremely boring. She took it as an example of his curious sense of humour. It might well have been, but I believe he also meant what he said.

I like to think he recognized me as a kindred spirit and that is why he allowed me a glimpse into the way he did things. His work was surprisingly structured. He had names for the different, clearly defined stages. It reminded me of a confidence trick.

The first was called 'The Put-back'. This lasted as long as he deemed necessary. It involved breaking into houses but rather than stealing anything, he would introduce an incongruous object. It might be a lady's left hand glove in the kitchen sink, a vase of roses in the fireplace or a broken clarinet in the toilet bowl. When he began to overhear people tell each other of the strange occurrences in their houses, he would move on to the next level that was called 'The Grooning'. This stage had a more communal aspect than the previous one, which was designed to work solely on individuals.

I witnessed it when I awoke one morning to discover thousands of oranges placed exactly one foot apart on every wall in the town. The deafeningly loud three second burst of a Johann Strauss waltz that seemed to come from nowhere, and the tripwire across the door of the Lutheran church were also examples of 'The Grooning'. These happenings would continue until Anton felt that the ground was suitably softened, then he would move on to the last stage, which he called 'Pelican Fury'.

This consisted of only one event and it happened on a Thursday. This was the day when everybody dressed as police officers. How he managed to pull off such a stunt, I cannot imagine. It was impressive. In one day we all became aware of how we were living. The next day Anton disappeared. He left a void but his impact lingered.

The police force of twenty-seven was cut by two thirds to nine—a more reasonable number. But the most extreme effect he had was the case of Rufus Williams, an eccentric millionaire. Immediately after Anton left, Williams began a controversial project called 'Purchase and Destroy'. He would buy up houses at market value and pay to have them demolished. He hoped to return the area to its virginal, pre-Columbian state. His activities continued until one day he was found dead in his car.

What became of Anton?

He went into the woods and hanged himself by the feet from a tree.

He went to another town that had a greater need than ours.

He is asleep in a cave.

He is in prison.

Italics

Mud, bishops and lovemaking. I am thinking about *L'Age d'Or,* that jagged film by Buñuel and Dali. I'm in the café I frequent practically every day. I sit in the corner and bury myself in my phone. That is what I use to write with. The gentle clatter and hubbub around me is conducive to writing, in a similar way perhaps to the use of white noise as a sleeping aid for some people. I can sit here and nurse a cup of coffee for hours without being moved on.

I had a flurry once, something that approximated motion towards success. I had two books published and I wrote some screenplays. With titles like 'Wedlock' and 'The History of the Chair', it's not surprising that they were never made. My agent is not much help as she suffers from the occupational hazard of drinking too much, too often. I've approached a few others, but I don't seem to be of any use to them, so I am sticking with Sally Newcombe for now.

I toy with the idea of not considering myself a writer, but just as someone who writes. Though there is no question of giving it up. It might be because it is inextricably knotted with my identity, or because its promise of reaching into another world is simply too alluring.

But that is all moot now because I am unable to write anything. I have nothing to say, and if I did I probably couldn't find the words or string them together. The problem is an existential one.

The phone is to blame. Socrates may have railed against literacy but Apple, intentionally or not, has set the course for the destruction of civilization as it has been conceived for millennia.

Either that or it has caused an accelerated evolution which has sent humanity careening towards existence as a digital machine. Maybe I am wrong, just trapped in my Luddite mind, but I used to carry a notebook and scribble feverishly. Now I carry a phone and the screed has become virtual, just an idea of writing, not writing itself. And now the spigot has completely seized up. Not a drop. It's like cancer of that gland. Pituitary gland? No. Which gland is it? It escapes me. Everything has gone.

Phone in hand I wait. There are thoughts but no purpose to them, no way they can be manipulated on to a page or screen. I have thrown a giraffe out of the window and kicked a violin down the street. I have shot someone for no reason. I have shaken back the oily quiff from my eyes. Now what?

Perhaps I should assume that I am a Celt. It makes sense. Those blue people had an insatiable need for sacrifice. A need so bad that they were inclined to sacrifice a victim three times—by garrotting, drowning and burning, or was it clubbing? The victim having chosen a piece of burnt bannock cake.

Those ancient people would have considered me decadent or deranged because, despite my entertaining fantasies, I don't like to kill anything. Still, they had other modes of sacrifice more appealing to me. They liked to throw things in water—valuable things into lakes or rivers. There is obviously something quintessentially human about that. The practice survives today as coins being tossed into fountains.

This form of sacrifice inspires me to fish a penny from my pocket and drop it into my half-full cup of tepid coffee. No sooner has it disappeared beneath the surface with a plop, than I think I hear a hiss. I watch as bubbles rise up from the bottom of the cup. They do not diminish but become more virulent until I realise that the liquid is boiling and emitting a large amount of steam. As the vapour gushes out, first the ambience and then the room itself disappear from my consciousness. A large person with a huge head stands before me. I can't determine whether it is male or female. I suspect that the head is covered by a wig of wild and straggly hair that reaches down to the shoulders.

"So you say you're a writer."

"I didn't say that."

"Well that's what you think. I know all your thoughts. I've been in your pocket. I'll be returning there soon."

"Who are you?"

"Winston Churchill. Have you ever thought that you are a clamourer, arrogant in your ignorance?"

I'm in the situation where good things to say come too late.

"You're not Winston Churchill."

"Nor are you. What of it? You're a second rate writer, a hack whose creations are so insignificant that even you can no longer believe in them. Yet you can't put them down. Your horse is dead but you persist in trying to ride it."

"What's your point?"

"I can put wings on your horse and breathe life back into its carcass. I can unblock your colon."

The large being in front of me has tears cascading down its bulbous cheeks.

"You're insulting me while offering to help, and you're crying. I don't understand."

"I'm not crying. I am ridding myself of excess fluid and I have no interest in helping you. What I'm offering is a proposition."

"Which is?"

"You want to write something good. I can make that happen. But it comes with a price."

I wanted to be able to write again. Quality was not yet a concern.

"And what do you charge for your services?"

"Whatever you write from now on, if you agree to my offer, will be italicized. That's not part of the fee. It's a parameter. The cost to you will be this—you will never write with pen or pencil on paper again. You will take the coin from your cup and put it back in your pocket. You will keep it there always. If you change your trousers the coin stays with you. Agreed?"

I reach for the pen I keep in my jacket.

"Do I have to sign?"

"No. If you renege, your newfound talents will shrivel faster than an old man's cock. No signature required."

With that, the being is gone and the café returns to normal, as if no time has passed. I scoop the coin out of the slimy dregs at the bottom of my coffee cup, wipe it off and put it in my pocket. I snap my pen in half and throw it away. From now on I will embrace my phone without misgivings.

Prostate. That's what that gland is. I feel clearer. I no longer need to meditate on the poster of the buxom farm woman with a basket of olives in her powerful arms or on the flaking paint on the wall beside her. A screenplay begins to form, faster than I had ever thought possible. My concentration is sharper than an obsidian knife. It is all flowing out in italics.

Within two weeks I've got a masterpiece. I'm not deluding myself this time. It's the best writing I've ever done. I have to get it out there. I call Sally.

"Hi Sally."

"Hold on."

I wait. The minutes seem like hours. There are some banging noises in the background.

"Yes?"

"It's me."

"Me? All people are 'me' to themselves. Who are you?"

"You know who I am. We lived together for five years."

Click.

In my enthusiasm I forgot to check the time. It's getting on for four-thirty. If you want to get anywhere with Sally it has to be earlier in the day.

The next morning I print a copy and take it over to her personally. I hand her the wad of paper. She is in her dressing gown, seated in her kitchen alcove. Flakes of croissant litter the table. She takes it from me and thumbs through it.

"The whole thing is in fucking italics."

"So?"

"What did you do that for?"

"I don't know. It just came out that way. Does it matter?"

"It's unprofessional, off-putting. I'm not going to read this in its current form. Give me another—without the italics."

She hands it back.

"I'm not sure I can do that."

I'd thought of this and tried to switch the tab before printing it. I'd attempted it on several different computers. Nothing worked. Even the copy shop couldn't do it. They told me the file was corrupted.

"You're not sure? What's wrong with you? Well, this may be as good a time as any to tell you. I've been thinking about our relationship. It's been stagnant for quite a while. You'd better look around for someone else. I can't help you anymore. Goodbye. And take that thing with you."

Bowing, Genuflection and Water

Ever since a chance encounter in the Tate gallery when he was about five years old, Jack Weir, whose eyes watered when confronted by authority, had been sensitive about bowing and genuflection.

His grandmother loved art and would traipse him around galleries. That day at the Tate she had spotted the Queen Mother and had told him to go forward and bow.

It was hot and stuffy. He was feeling tired and overwhelmed. The paintings had become irritating. He unwillingly complied because she did not accept any breaches of discipline.

So he made his way through the crowd of legs and bowed before the Royal person. The Queen Mother looked down at him from her big flowery hat and gave a lovely smile. She was everyone's grandmother, he realised later, and always appeared to be the same age up until her death—if in fact she had really died at all.

When he was older he met a woman on a beach who studied human movement. She wasn't concerned so much with mechanics but psychology. It had sounded odd at first but began to seem less strange as she explained how the way people walked spoke volumes about their individual psychological states as well as their more collective cultural aspects—Americans trod differently than Vietnamese.

Today a course on the psychology of movement seems very much an expression of its time. Yet it complemented his ideas on bowing and genuflection which had always been a strange background noise to his life.

That long-gone conversation had nourished the seed

embedded at the Tate so many years before. Occidental and Oriental bowing had different forms which were an expression of a deep cultural disparity but they were still bowing nonetheless. A vine began to grow. Its shoots rose quickly.

Jack Weir was very familiar with water. He listened to it coursing below the city streets almost every day through a hollow stick with an earpiece attached. His job as a Water Board inspector caused him to bend sideways. This did not constitute a bow. He had thought about it often as subterranean rivers filled his ear—unless there was such a thing as a sideways bow. But a lateral bend would not conform to the essence of the forward abasement. In fact it would be its opposite, a sign of disrespect. That made him laugh, and he vowed to himself that should he ever meet a queen or king again he would bow sideways.

Bowing was a symbol of deference, whether the head was lowered to avert a challenging gaze or to receive a blow. Yet it was an act of submission rooted somehow in the animal kingdom. Such ritual submission might help to diminish violence. What rankled Jack was the ubiquity of dominance and subjugation in most species of animals. This fragile human civilization was dependent on it and constantly threatened by it at the same time. Leaders, both feared and revered, must always have been lacking some mental faculty which made cooperation, and therefore civilization possible. They might be seen as malfunctioning individuals. They might be treated in a gene-splicing clinic.

There was a leak. He could hear it. He straightened himself and clutched his stick under one arm as the other reached for the notebook in his pocket. It was a cumbersome procedure, as his jacket was made from a material so stiff he might as well have been clothed in wood. But he was used to it.

Some people even lay down. That was on the extreme end of the spectrum. And then of course there was genuflection, usually but not exclusively reserved for certain religious practices. A kneeling person would be virtually unable to defend himself. A very suitable arrangement.

With this final leak recorded, his day's work was done and he headed home. He stopped on the way for a pint. One pint led to another and then there was a sleepy train ride. It was still light when he let himself in, fumbling for his keys in a pocket that felt unwelcoming. He glanced at his dowsing rods—two fine sticks of willow jammed in with the umbrellas at the bottom of the coat stand. He added his listening tube to the collection.

"Have you been drinking?"

Her voice came from the kitchen which had no door.

"I just had one."

It seemed to him that after twenty years of marriage, conversation had become a legal deposition.

"Only one?"

"Yes."

He abruptly kept going and went upstairs to change out of his work clothes.

"There's some food for you on the counter."

He was already hanging up his clothes in the wardrobe, and as he shouted back his thanks he thought perhaps he would dispense with food and go out dowsing. Some people amused themselves with metal detectors, seeking to unearth treasure from the ground but he enjoyed the silent excitement of the rods dancing in his hands. He knew he had a way with water. It was a solitary experience for which there was no valid scientific explanation. But it seemed to work. Though he never bothered to dig down and find the water he had divined, the rods would always bend.

As he grabbed the willows and left the house, June was talking to someone on the phone which made his exit more fluid. He meandered in a leisurely way, his wands twitching occasionally until he reached the river where they bent violently to his great satisfaction.

Later, as he turned on to his street on the way home, he saw two policemen get out of their car.

"Excuse me Sir."

"Yes."

"You live around here, do you?"

"Yes. Why?"

"There's been a burglary."

"So?"

"There were footprints. Lift up your foot. Let me see the sole of your shoe. Looks like mud. What do you think Dave?"

"Looks like mud to me."

"Shoe size looks the same too, and the print matches. Do you own a dog?"

"No."

"Are you sure about that?"

He didn't like the way most people assumed that animals were mere chattels.

"I have never owned a dog."

Damn these eyes. They were watering copiously.

"Are you all right Sir? Do you need a handkerchief?"

The second officer, the one called Dave, was looking at him with a mocking smile. Then the first one cut in again:

"What are you doing with those sticks?"

"They're dowsing rods."

"Oh, dowsing for water are we?"

The two policemen looked puzzled. Perhaps it didn't make sense to them, though they knew there must be a reason. Or perhaps it was just that they did not like to admit their error—neither to him nor to themselves. They moved away from him and closer to each other.

"Have you been drinking?"

"No. I don't drink."

"Do you take any medications?"

"No."

"On your way then."

He could feel them watching him as he walked down the street. He felt self-conscious and guilty, as if he had committed a crime. He wondered what the woman on the beach would have made of his gait. It was strange that they suspected him, a middle-aged man, of robbery. The experience was disturbing.

Things might have turned out differently. They could have easily arrested him, and the machinery of justice would have begun to grind without him ever knowing what he was supposed to have done. The kind of thing Franz Kafka wrote about.

He cursed his condition of watering eyes. If the eyes were the window to the soul, then his soul had betrayed him again and again. But he found the concept of 'soul' rather vague. It was more that his watery eyes were a reminder of an inherent quality in people—one of those archaic mechanisms that transcended species and caused patterns of behaviour like bowing and genuflection, so obscure that their purpose had long since vanished.

It was a good thing that the dog he had befriended and which had accompanied him all the way down to the river, had wandered off when he passed the housing estate at the top of his road.

The Tennis Court

The tennis court—bisected by a stiff net, with lines drawn on the ground. Who is to say it does not have a forgotten significance other than the obvious one?

He sat down on the bench and looked around him. Weeds had broken through the asphalt and climbed between the warped and lichened slats. The court stretched out on either side of him, empty and decayed. The cordage of the net was frayed and its tautness had relaxed into a sway-backed droop, but its presence suggested that tennis was still played there on occasion. He wondered what that occasion might be.

He had come upon this place while walking in the woods. There was a clearing in the trees and an embankment, then a tennis court in the forest. It had drawn him down. He had followed the lines, faint but still extant, as they described a series of rectangles on the ground. They gave him an inkling that there was something more to all of this, something overlooked. Such angular geometrical shapes, nothing like the curves and imperfections found in nature, had to be an attempt to impose order on chaos. Boundaries were common to all ball games, as was the idea of the ball in motion. He could not think of any game which required a static ball.

After circumnavigating the court, he went in turn to both ends of it. He gazed over the net and beyond, trying to see with the eyes of a player. The soft light from an overcast sky filtered down through the leafy chlorophyll. He saw that this ubiquitous greenness faded to black beyond the boundary line at each end of the court. Humanity had once lived out there in the shade. It was a place they had shared with other ferocious mammals. Life was most likely tenuous and short. And so, in an act which

143

raised themselves out of the food chain, they had invented the game of tennis. More accurately, tennis was merely one result in an evolution of ball games over millennia.

The ball must always be kept in motion. It was propelled originally by the naked hand, then by a racket, itself an extension of the hand, and harbinger of the industrial era.

There were rules, limitations of necessity which reduced the cacophonous complexities of life to a scale that could be managed by humans. The ball, so important to keep aloft, was allowed to bounce once. The bounce had a curious significance. If the purpose of the game was to create a model of life's dynamics, and then to influence or control them, in a way analogous to sympathetic magic, then the bounce might be seen as a flirtation with death. Its inclusion in the rules only made the model more vivid, and the magic more effective. It could be that the purpose of tennis was only for enjoyment, or for keeping fit. There is no reason why these purposes should not all run concurrently. They are not mutually exclusive.

As it travelled across the court, bouncing or not, the ball created a waveform, its length being determined by the distance between rackets. He suspected there was a special significance to this, perhaps a way to experience every game that had ever been played. The accumulation of such waveforms in a match would provide a distinctive colophon. He could not know for sure. It was an idea, nothing more.

At that point he had sat down on the bench. He did not believe in any of these thoughts. He considered it an arrogant fallacy to assume that one is obligated to believe one's thoughts. Belief is completely irrelevant.

In the woods beyond the court, were trees in the process of falling. Some were already on the ground, dark and rotting. Others leant on their siblings. There was no breeze and no movement, except for a woodpecker furiously tapping nearby.

Billie Jean King, Jimmy Connors, Arthur Ashe, Chris Evert, Andy Murray, Bjorn Borg, Rod Laver, Henry VIII, John McEnroe, Pete Sampras, Venus Williams, Andy Roddick, Gavin

Tranent, Rafael Nadal, Serena Williams, Andre Agassi, Roger Federer, Maria Sharapova.

He recited the names of the tennis players he could recall. All of them were known to the world. These people engaged their bodies in a perpetual struggle for the betterment of humanity. Civilization was not something that could be attained once, and then appreciated for time ever after. It had to be maintained constantly. Winning was not as important as delaying the inevitable.

He leaned back on the bench and stretched out his legs, heels down, toes up. His mildly depressing metaphysics had made him thirsty. The crumbling dryness of the court, offered no relief. Nature was reclaiming it, with no concern for him. He thought somehow that if only he could watch a few games he would feel better. It would be an opportunity to test the waveform idea. But how to determine amplitude? Would the point of equilibrium be the centre between the ground and the highest position of the ball, or its median height, in any given shot? None of the information was available to him. It was an analogy made from science that belonged in the realm of pseudo-science, more use perhaps in art than to him now.

If he was to watch a game, he was going to have to think one up himself. He stayed where he was. Nothing but silence and emptiness. He was trying too hard. Not complete silence, because he could hear the sounds of birds and insects, quite clearly, more than before, he realised. The majority of these sounds were the noises of eating, on a huge scale. It was as if the world around him was being devoured.

"Advantage Thundrel."

The game was already in play and had reached a moment of tension. He was looking to his left and saw the man about to receive the serve. It was Gavin Tranent, standing with legs apart and slightly bent at the knee, nervously twirling his racket with his right hand. At the other end of the court, his opponent was flexing to serve. It was shocking to see Thundrel toss up the ball and drive it over the net with unimaginable force. Greasy hair flew back from both of his massive heads which towered above the trees behind him. Watching from the bench, he spun around to see how Tranent, who was of normal stature, would survive the serve. Remarkably, gripping the racket with both hands, he returned the ball, causing it to skim just above the net and drop to the ground almost instantly. Thundrel stumbled and lost the point. In this case his two heads appeared to work against him. Both of them had lost the confident, malevolent grins of the moment before, when he had thought the game was his, and were now set in anxious scowls.

"Deuce."

The ball was already in Tranent's section of the court when he heard the boom, meaning that the projectile had surpassed the speed of sound. With an adroit feint, he suddenly turned an apparent back hand swing to a forehand, sending the ball in an unexpected direction, which perplexed the giant.

"Advantage Tranent."

Thundrel was now enraged and the sweat was dripping copiously from his brows. It must have been noon, the sky had cleared and the sun was directly overhead, burning off the green light. Tranent, oddly but understandably clothed in body armour, seemed lithe and full of energy.

Thundrel flubbed the serve twice. His anger had broken his concentration. His last attempt ripped a hole through the net.

"Game, set and match, Gavin Tranent. Two sets to one. Four-six, six-love, six-four."

The giant Thundrel turned and smashed his racket on the ground. He was a bad loser, showing no inclination to the honour code of sportsmen, either in victory or defeat, and abruptly strode off into the forest. He plucked up trees as he went and snapped them like matches in his great fists.

There was a ten minute break before the next match. This was to be a bout between Tranent and Ysbaddaden, a giant from Wales. Tranent leaned against a chair which had been brought on to the court for him. An assistant raised his vizor and held a chalice to his lips.

When the rest period was over, Tranent made short work of

Ysbaddaden, who was old and slow. The afternoon drew on. He defeated three more Welsh Giants and a Scandinavian. His strategy had been the same all day—keep the ball close to the ground and to the bodies of his opponents, causing them to bend, and preventing them from using their full strength in a swing.

The ball was sized on a human scale, no doubt to compensate for the vastly superior strength of the giants. To them it would have appeared no larger than a marble or a pea. This was a disadvantage, considering their poor eyesight.

Jack-in-Irons appeared to be a formidable foe, all draped in chains and human heads. But he was more image than substance, and Tranent defeated him without much difficulty. By now, as the evening approached he was visibly flagging. It was not surprising, considering his day-long exertions, but the man on the bench could not stop himself from wondering if Tranent derived his almost super-human strength from sunlight.

His last adversary of the day, and the seventeenth, was Gogmagog. He was a minor celebrity among tennis-playing giants and made Tranent suffer horribly. For the winning shot in a tie-breaking game, Tranent summoned his remaining vigour and drove the ball as powerfully as he could between the giant's legs, just below his presumably monstrous organs of generation. Gogmagog got tangled up in his own body and was unable to parry.

The tournament was over. Most of the giants went away and became mountains. The Welsh ones certainly did. Tranent lay supine and shuddering on the court. His assistants were frantically pouring water into his helmet. He had done his duty for mankind, because after that day, humanity was never again bothered by that alternate and problematic species.

He raised himself off the bench with sleeping buttocks. It must be time to pick up his daughter from her dancing class. He left the court and climbed the embankment. Would it be possible to introduce a ball to the game of chess? It could be called Chessball. How would it work? Of course—this might be the perfect opportunity for the first game with a static ball.

The Buried Queen

A queen was buried beneath the threshold. Jenny had been stepping over it for years without knowing what lay below. Builders had made the discovery while digging down to repair the foundations.

It was a pivotal moment in a subtle way, a growing awareness of what she didn't know. It spread through her like cracks in a window pane.

She suspected that most people thought she led a boring existence. Friends and strangers alike were always telling her that she should move to London. Opportunities were so much greater there. She could find a better job, make more money and meet more people. She could continue her education. She was wasting herself in this place.

Jenny found this advice oppressive. It was well intended but unsolicited and patronizing. Most of it came from people whose houses she cleaned, usually affluent Londoners with second homes. They spoke to her with preconceived notions and without acknowledging her own choice in the matter. It might be true that there were more opportunities in London but that didn't mean she wanted to live there. She had her reasons for staying where she was. Though it was true she hadn't had a formal education, she had educated herself by reading avidly and following her interests. None of this occurred to them. They didn't know she had a deep continuity with this place. People who were unfamiliar with where their great grandparents had lived could never understand it.

Her family had occupied their house for close to seven hundred years. They must have moved in round about the time of Poitiers. She lived there still. That familial continuity with place was very important to her. It gave her a strong feeling of depth and belonging, and she experienced time as more of a continuum than most people did. To advise her to move away would be like telling her to get a limb amputated. She never talked about these things but just listened and kept her thoughts to herself.

She had often wondered how it was that her family had managed to stay in the same house for all those years, and how the house itself had managed to survive. It was so unusual. She had never met anyone with a similar experience. When she was younger she had been embarrassed by it, as it made her feel different. Now, at twenty-seven, she was more self-assured and didn't care so much what other people thought.

Generations of her family had been born and died in the house. Some had moved away. Those who left were the ones who had suffered the most bad luck as far as she could tell. There was her great-great uncle Geoffrey Wilkins who had gone to Australia in the 1870s to seek his fortune. He had died drunk in a stable, having fallen from a hayloft. Her grandmother's cousin Janice had moved with her husband to London, probably to benefit from the opportunities it offered, only to succumb to a German bomb in the Second World War. In the mid 1600s Samuel Wilkins went to live in London with his branch of the family. They all perished in the plague of 1665. Moving away did not seem a good idea—especially not to London.

The family members who had stayed behind blurred into each other over time. They had led unremarkable lives, just as most people do, absorbed by the mundanities of existence with its sorrows and pleasures. Except that in her family's case they also had a personal awareness of the past. She had the sense that she was grasping a frayed string that dipped downwards through the centuries. If she pulled it, she wondered, following the metaphor—what would come up? She imagined an old medieval leather bucket containing a single treasure, sloshing in the water.

The house had changed over the generations with numerous additions and renovations. All that remained of the original structure was part of the kitchen and an adjoining room. The medieval hovel had become cocooned in a sprawling, rambling succession of building upon building. The wild and unkempt garden at the back of the house was the only remaining private expanse of green in the area, for the old village had rapidly become a town in the 1980s.

After they discovered the queen, whose hand still rested upon her face, the builders found a bishop lying nearby. He was holding a broken crook. Both of them were perfectly preserved. Archaeologists soon got wind of it.

The figures, both about nine centimetres high, were made from a mixture of plaster and resin, most likely cast from a medieval mould, now lost. They resembled the pieces from the famous York set. The consensus among the archaeologists was that the pieces had been made and buried sometime between 1810 and 1820. They were obviously used as talismans to ward off evil spirits. This kind of folk magic was apparently quite common at the time, especially in rural areas. The placement below the threshold underscored the point, as everyone always knew that evil entered a house through its doorways.

After the discovery Jenny read up on the game of chess to satisfy her curiosity. Chess was really the first game to completely dispense with chance. Even backgammon, which required some skill to play well, required a throw of dice to dictate the moves. Chess was pure strategy. In the Middle Ages there had been a European variation of the game that incorporated dice, as if the abandonment of chance was not initially acceptable. The idea of pure strategy might have been an alien concept in the feudal era. Perhaps the significance of chance had been to represent what was uncontrollable in life. Games have a way of modelling a larger reality. The simple game of snakes and ladders concerned the teaching of morality.

The leap from the chessboard to the realm of spirits was also a strategic act, and not unreasonable. It seemed to her to be quite advanced despite its air of superstition. That was because it was a shifting of concepts, a spate of neural reconnections, similar in a way to the orthodox, popular tale of the discovery of DNA. A shape seen in a dream became that well-known double helix.

Jenny had always imagined that grand masters of chess plotted moves in advance and were able to keep in their minds the myriad possibilities and variations dependent on the actions of the other player. But possibilities in chess rapidly increase exponentially as the game progresses, soon becoming so numerous that no human brain could ever contain them all. So it appeared that grand masters kept an image of the board in their minds, a dynamic image equivalent to an Impressionist painting. She liked this idea of a shimmering image to describe how the chess pieces became talismans, slipping unnoticed from one state to another.

The archaeologists had said that the bishop and queen were the obvious choices for talismans because of their religious significance. She could accept that opinion for the bishop but was not so sure about the queen. Her family had been Protestant since the Reformation, so the queen as the mother of Christ would not have held the same significance for them as she would have done for Catholics. She might have represented an older female deity but Jenny suspected it was their capacity for movement in the game that had something to do with it. Both queen and bishop were powerful pieces. Who would want to use a king as a talisman?

The game of chess might nominally be about attacking or defending the king but the king himself was weak, virtually powerless, a prisoner almost. He was not much more than an aggrandized pawn. This might be another example, she thought, of how chess can transcend realities, considering the caliber of contemporary politicians.

At least the king had a face. The pawns in the York set were tombstones, faceless, not even human. Chess could make a social comment too. Her ancestors might have been among those pawns, pulling back bowstrings on the battlefields of the Hundred Years War.

Another interesting thing Jenny had learned from reading about chess, was that the queen had undergone a gender change. She didn't start out as female. Chess was likely to have originated in India and came into Europe through Spain with the Arab conquest. At the time the queen was male and known as the vizier. Then perhaps in honour of Queen Isabella I of Castile, the vizier changed sex and became a queen. It was a transition full of inference when viewed from a modern perspective. The most powerful piece was trans-gender but Jenny chose to see it as a milestone in women's long crawl from 'chatteldom' towards equality—still underway.

If the archaeologists had got the dating right, then her great-great-great-great grandmother Sarah would have buried the pieces. Intuitively she knew it was a woman who had done this. Women kept the family history alive and passed it down through generations. She was a part of that herself.

It occurred to her that there could have been no intention at all. Sarah might have dropped a couple of pieces while clearing up after the children who had been playing outside. Over time they might have worked their way under the house. But assuming that the pieces were deliberately used as talismans, then why were they placed there at that time?

In 1815 the Corn Laws were passed, keeping grain prices high. This benefited the producers but hurt consumers, especially the lowly ones. In 1816 there was a famine caused by a volcanic eruption in Indonesia. It was the year of winter, harvests were bad and the situation became critical. There were riots in London. This was a time of stress and might explain why Sarah buried the talismans when she did.

Then Jenny had a minor epiphany. She was thinking about the Great Wall of China and that she had heard its purpose was not only to keep barbarians out but to keep citizens in. She asked herself why it was that the buried queen was there to ward off evil and not to keep goodness from seeping out.

And then it hit her—Sarah was not trying to prevent evil from entering the house. She was trying to keep her family together at a time when tensions were high and it could have easily broken apart. In other words she had bewitched the family to keep the love in. It was quite likely the process had been going on for centuries and that there were many more artefacts to be found buried on the property. That was why the family had managed to stay together for so long in the same place.

Now, the chess pieces had been taken away to undergo various tests. Jenny didn't have a good feeling about it. She told one of the archaeologists her theory about the talismans being used to contain things rather than to exclude them, omitting the personal details. He wasn't much older than she was. He said it was an interesting idea and then, raising an eyebrow:

"You know, you should think about moving. An intelligent woman like you. Maybe to London... there's nothing for you here."

Perhaps he was right. There seemed to be an entropic force towards homogeneity that was becoming more and more difficult to resist. Sooner or later she would have to move. The house would be torn down and replaced with a block of flats. Her family would disappear, merging into the rest of humanity.

Freedom from Belief

A policemen pulled me over. I was driving my car from the back seat and had made an illegal turn.

"Who do you think you are?" He asked me, "Alice in Wonderland?"

But he let me go without giving me a ticket and then I woke up. I ran my hands through my hair, feeling my skull. Its topography gently dipped and rose beneath my fingers. I really had to brush up on phrenology. Maybe I could learn something. It was a discredited science of course, if it had ever been a science, but it had its uses. Unexpected possibilities can arise from relaxing into the luxury of error.

Glimpses of how people thought in earlier times, especially when those thoughts were now rejected with amazement, can elucidate the preposterousness of some of our contemporary beliefs. They can suggest that cultural bias is inherent in nearly every idea. To acknowledge one's own prejudice is to raise oneself through abstraction and is a step towards freedom from belief—an imaginary state of being where one can meld oneself with the essence of life, if there is such a thing. It is of course unattainable, something to approach but never reach.

But still, phrenology has its uses.

As I washed my face and cleaned my teeth, I shot a quick glance into the mirror. I could see the bathroom window and beyond it to the sky pierced by treetops. I looked again at my other self. Being dark haired, thick browed, with eyes set further apart than most people's, I would obviously once have been considered a criminal, even though I had not yet committed any crimes worth prosecuting as far as I knew.

My job as an emergency medical technician, subjected me daily to the rawest of situations where I witnessed humanity shorn of its trappings. I spent my time helping people but it was not without cost. Constant exposure to such a pure form of reality left me with a feeling of solitude. I functioned and did my duty with an adequate degree of professionalism but I was disengaged.

I imagine my colleagues felt the same way, though nothing much was said. Occasionally we would go out together to celebrate a birthday and the festivities would be taken to the limit, or to the edge of it. It seemed to me that this crowd of revellers was a collection of solitudes, temporarily ignored but not forgotten. No wonder we sought oblivion.

Today, however, was my day off and I did not have to witness anything I did not wish to see. As I dried my face, I wondered about what would constitute a perfect crime. It would obviously have to be something that was not recognized as a crime. Would it be a murder in which the victim was not even harmed? Would it be a theft in which the stolen object was returned before it was known to be missing? It was a conundrum. These theoretically criminal acts would not actually be crimes, and I found myself back where I started.

I caught my eye in the mirror and saw the flash of recognition. The answer was obvious. The perfect crime would be committed in the looking-glass world.

The problem with the perfect crime was the concept itself. To qualify a crime as 'perfect' was to buy into that figment of culture which idealized a certain narrow bracket of individualism, played out again and again in all media, from Moriarty to heist films. In that respect it only reinforced the status quo where self-made individuals could deny to themselves their dependence on the state they eschewed. It represented everything I was trying to escape from.

He looked again to the mirror, half-hoping to see Ayn Rand on horseback among the tumbleweeds of the Southwest. But he only saw himself, shifty and turning away because he did not like these kind of confrontations.

156

With a jolt, I realized I had been thinking about myself in the third person. Unless it was my reflection who had been thinking about me. We were entangled like photons—I and I.

The question was if there was any autonomy, or whether we were bound to do exactly the same things, just flipped on the vertical axis. At first this vertical flip seemed like an important difference until I thought about water swirling down drains in the antipodes. Then it seemed no more remarkable than different shades of green among the leaves of trees or different faces on the street. But still, if a reflection was conscious, how would a flip of the vertical axis affect thought? They were too disparate to connect. Would it be akin to reverse polarity? That was easier to grasp.

I hung up my towel. Time to go out. I spoke to the mirror.

"Goodbye. I'll see you later."

It was an awkward moment, excruciatingly self-conscious. The words were mouthed back at me with no sound. That was the difference—light not sound.

When he finally left I was able to relax again. At last peace. He had a heaviness about him, a philosophical yearning that went nowhere. It was emotionally draining. I heard him go out. Not sure where, but he wasn't driving. I could tell that. He probably went for something to eat.

That left me wondering what to do with myself all day. Aside from certain obligations I did pretty much whatever I wanted. He was an ambulance driver. Fuck that. I decided it would be fun to go and visit his girlfriend, to see if she could tell the difference between us. Good for a laugh. At least for a while. He was bound to be over at some point. A man of habit, though he didn't know it. Pathetic really.

It wasn't far to her house. I rang the bell. She came down to let me in.

"You're early. Don't you have your keys?"

"I must have left them at home."

"But they're on your key ring. The one I gave you. Didn't you drive?"

"*No. I walked.*" *God this woman was annoying—relentless.* "*I'm trying to cut down on my carbon emissions.*"

I followed her up the stairs to her living room.

"*Do you want some coffee?*"

"*Yes.*"

While she was clattering around in the kitchen I noticed a wad of money on the bookshelf, so I took it. Why not? Her watch was there too, the one he must have given her. I took that as well.

She came back in and set the coffee before me.

"*What should we do today?*"

"*I don't know. Do you want to have sex?*"

"*Are you out of your mind? What's come over you? I know your job stresses you out but this is your day off. If you think you can just walk in here and demand sex, maybe you should think again. Or just go home.*"

While she was carrying on, I got up and looked out of the window. This wasn't as fun as I had hoped. What did he see in her? He wasn't exactly a fool but he certainly was an idiot.

"*John.*"

Damn. There he was now. I could see him parking below.

"*John... what's the matter with you? Aren't you listening? Have you forgotten your name?*"

I turned. I didn't have a name myself. I didn't know his name and I had no idea what she was called. Names were completely unimportant to me. They just seemed like sentimental, other-worldly rubbish.

"*What?*"

"*Have you seen my watch?*"

"*No. Hold on...*" *I made a dash to the stairs.*

"*Where are you going?*"

"*I'll be right back.*"

I slipped out, leaving the front door open and just avoiding him before he came around the corner. This whole thing had been a waste of time. Still, I was going to leave him in some deep water. There was pleasure in that. As I walked along the street, the thought of deep water gave me a good idea.

When I got home I knew something was wrong right away. First I heard it, then I saw it. Water was gushing from the ceiling. I rushed to the bathroom. The tub and sink were plugged and all the taps were on. There was water everywhere. It must have been running for hours. The place was ruined. Who could have done this? The door was locked and there was no sign of a break-in.

I waded across the floor and turned off the taps. I'd go down and get the wet and dry vacuum and see what I could do about cleaning up some of this water. Tomorrow I would take the day off and call the insurance company. I should probably file a police report right away. Tonight I would have to stay at Sarah's place, if she would have me. It had been difficult, and that was an understatement. She had been quite crazy, thinking that I had been there when I hadn't, and being angry with me about it.

Before leaving the bathroom I looked at myself in the mirror, it was hard not to look into it in this enclosed space. But there was no reflection of me, just the room and the window behind where I should have been standing. No. There I was, looking haggard. What was happening to me? Could it be some kind of cognitive dysfunction related to stress? Could I have turned on the water myself and gone to Sarah's before I thought I did? Was she right?

Tomorrow it would be the doctor as well as the insurance company.

That was the obligation I was talking about. Every time he looked into the mirror, I had to be there too. It was a magnetic attraction. There was nothing I could do about it. I had been sleeping one moment, and the next I was forced to stare into his ugly face. He had the dominance in this situation. That's why I got back at him every time I could...

Antifoni

"The moon is winking at me through the clouds."

Stuva Grundlig stood on a bluff overlooking the sea. This was a sign, this winking moon. Tomorrow they would go. They had been ready for three weeks, but during that time there had never been a correct moment. He had been waiting impatiently and keeping everyone else on tenterhooks. The sign in the dark sky above him was neither favourable nor malign, but it beckoned and he could not resist. Stuva was bearded and powerfully built, with a weakness that made him susceptible to exciting propositions. So this was it. Tomorrow they would leave.

He was sick of this town and its shoddy buildings. It had been rapidly deteriorating. A period of unusually persistent and heavy rain had caused it to flake and buckle. So much for permanence, he thought. You can't find it here. He dreamed of cities made from stone. Affordable housing was no excuse for compressed cardboard.

Snorri Rimforsa had watched with amused curiosity as Grundlig built his boat. He had done it out in the open, in front of his ramshackle house. It had been completed quite quickly in just under two months, and had been sitting on its rollers ever since. Grundlig had worked on it tirelessly through the daylight hours. He occasionally had help from Hektar and Jänsjo, and from some other malcontents.

Stuva Grundlig was unabashedly vocal about his ideas, which usually involved masonry and the merits of stone houses. He had become the unofficial voice of the disaffected—their tribune in a way.

He had constructed the hull of his boat from ferrous concrete.

Where he had managed to get the steel from was anyone's guess, as real metal was hard to come by these days. What was readily available were alloys, which seemed to grow lighter every year. Snorri wondered if there was not some secret process which made possible the melding of metals and plastics. The plastic component seemed to increase with time.

He was beginning to sound like Grundlig.

Snorri Rimforsa was a retired policeman. He had joined the force young, had done his twenty years, and now still in his forties, was able to lead a modest but comfortable existence in the small house over the road from his boat-building neighbour.

The off-white hull glistened. Grundlig must have oiled or painted it with a sealant. Snorri had watched him sand it down for hours at a time until the surface was perfectly smooth. He had to admit that Grundlig had done an excellent job. Despite the more anarchic aspects of his character, he had a single-minded focus that enabled him to do everything well. He had always been that way, even as a boy. They had grown up together, not far from where they were now.

People were arriving at Grundlig's house. Vårvind came around the corner and acknowledged him as he passed. Hektar and Jänsjo were already there. Snorri was sitting on his porch. His policeman's eye, still sharp after all these years, took in the goings-on across the street.

The door clattered shut. Grundlig was coming down the path towards the boat. He was carrying a heavy barrel with Stentorp. They heaved it over the gunwale, laughing and swearing. Grundlig looked happy.

Snorri recognized most of the people who kept showing up over the road. He had crossed paths with a few in the course of his work. It was a close-knit community and even if you did not know someone personally, then the chances were you had heard of them.

He didn't like Stentorp. He had questioned him once over a theft. Nothing had come of it. Stentorp had left the area after that, and had been gone for eight years. That was an admission of guilt, if anything was. There was a callowness to him, despite his age, and a dishonesty caused by fear. He had bluster but it wasn't bolstered by courage. If you challenged him, he would back down.

Valentina came out next. She was Grundlig's wife, more formidable than her husband, big, red-headed and strong. She lugged a bulging sack down the path and swung it into the boat. There were two men on board who received it, Strandmon and Preben. Grundlig was barking instructions to them in his stentorian voice, on how to stow the load. He had the even distribution of weight in mind.

From his porch, Snorri watched them work. It was a small boat. He counted thirteen rowing benches. Grundlig had built a *karve*. What could he be up to? There was a name painted in red near the prow. He strained his eyes to read it—Antifoni.

He hadn't noticed this before. It must have been a recent addition. He wondered what Grundlig was trying to say by using this name. It implied a call and response. Snorri had the sense that Grundlig had been shouting into the wind, a man alone with his ideas. But now the gathering of people in his garden was the response he needed. It created a completeness, where a multitude of disparate parts became aware of each other and functioned as one, resulting in a higher level of meaning than any one of them could have provided alone. It was a completeness usually associated with music—hence the name. Snorri could see that this was a turning point, where thought became action, and it was all centred upon the boat.

The vessel was now loaded and Grundlig stood with a large bottle of wine in his hands, surrounded by his shipmates. Snorri started to count them. It was tricky as they kept moving around, but after several attempts he settled on the number twenty-six, including Grundlig, who still held the unopened bottle. He seemed to be waiting for something.

What he was waiting for became apparent presently when Örfjäll shuffled into the yard. He was probably the strangest person in the town, barely half the height of most men. He wore a sleeveless leather coat. A raven was tethered to a ring on his shoulder. The bird had slashed his right cheek with its talons and shat down his back, but he was unperturbed. He was tough through and through. No pretence.

That quality of toughness was no doubt honed by the necessities of survival. Beyond it was another quality, much more nefarious and hard to describe. He seemed to have the ability to look into other places—those not bound by the physical world. You would never have known it from his weather-beaten face and foul mouth, but if you became familiar with him, you could detect it—in his stance, or in his eyes, or even in the odd word that punctuated his curses.

Once Örfjäll had joined them, Grundlig relaxed and brought a closed fist down on the little man's head with a burst of laughter. Then he pulled the cork from the bottle and slugged it down. He passed it around and everyone took a swig. Eventually the bottle found its way back to him. He tipped it upside down and spilled the remaining contents on the ground, then he suddenly hurled it against his house. It bounced off a wall and fell unbroken to the grass.

Everyone then set to pushing the boat out into the road, and down to the sea. Normally such boats would be carried, but not this one. There was a frantic scrambling to bring the exposed rollers at the stern forward, and place them under the bow, before the vessel was grounded. Six people prevented it from gaining too much momentum by pulling on ropes.

As they passed his house, Grundlig broke away and came up to the porch.

"You should leave your boring life behind, Snorri, and come with us."

"Where are you going?"

"We're abandoning this shit hole."

"But what's your destination?"

"We are going to a better place."

He paused and looked down to the water.

164

"Better to die at sea than in a cardboard box. Are you coming?"

"No, Stuva. I like my boring existence. I'm staying here. But good luck."

Without another word, Grundlig shrugged and turned back to his companions. Soon they had the ship afloat and waded out to board it. Someone tossed Örfjäll into the boat and he took his position as rudder man, in the stern. The raven on his shoulder stood out starkly against the overcast sky. The rowers readied themselves on the benches and took up their oars. They held them up parallel to the water, making the Antifoni bristle as she drifted out into the bay.

Grundlig stood in the prow, gazing majestically into the distance. Then he stepped out, on to the raised oars on the leeward side, facing the shore. Snorri watched as he leaped nimbly between them in a dance which tempted fate. He traversed the length of the boat twice, then climbed back aboard. The oars dropped into the water and the Antifoni disappeared out to sea.

They never came back.

Six years passed. Patches of grey appeared on Snorri's temples. He still liked to sit on his porch in the mornings and look out to sea, from his new stone house that occupied exactly the same position as his old one.

In a twist of irony, not long after Grundlig had departed with his crew, a new municipal authority had decreed that the previous experiments with cardboard had been an abject failure. A new town was built from stone. It was possible that Grundlig's ranting had been heard from above. He should have stayed. Or perhaps Snorri should have taken him up on his offer and gone with him.

He shared his house now, with Utrusta and their young son Stuva. As he aged, his thoughts were frequently drawn to the fate of The Antifoni, and her crew of brave or stupid men, and one woman.

He tried to remember their names:

Örfjäll, Docksta, Svartäsen, Vårvind, Sinnerlig, Ranarp,

Lagrad, Ribba, Synas, Trofast, Lixhult...
There were more, but they had all gone now.

The Chalice

It had something to do with a submarine and a chalice. It was meant to be an explanation but had the opposite effect. She spoke in an obscure language. He tried to keep up. The gist of it all concerned the dispossessed and those who had never possessed. How their numbers were creeping, as their fingers slipped from every building, every street, every open space, defined by exclusion. The opposite of reaching.

They were sitting in an apartment on the eleventh floor of a new tower. One of those buildings that were springing up like dragons' teeth all over New York City where air rights were the next frontier. A new way to monetize emptiness.

The apartment was large and decorated crisply in a modern style. It was comfortable but self-conscious in its minimalism. The ceilings were higher than the standard eight feet and large windows overlooked Fifth Avenue.

He was on the sofa, one leg stretched out and the other crossing it casually. She was sitting on the rug in a mystical oriental style, the soles of her bare feet turned upwards and nestled in her crotch. She had been talking for five hours.

On the window sill stood a vase of peonies, surrounded by their fallen petals. They filled the room with an aroma that suggested something delicious. He let his eyes rest on them absentmindedly as he grappled with the meaning of the submarine. He began to free associate—underwater, submersible, periscope, deceptive, hidden, seabed, the Antikythera mechanism, lost cities of the deep, Atlantis. Each generation of words took him further from the source. His gaze slipped beyond the vase and to the street below.

What he saw in the street snapped him from his reverie instantly. The whole of Fifth Avenue, the entire roadway and both sidewalks, was jammed with people shoulder to shoulder for as far as he could see. The people were so tightly packed, there was room for nothing else. The double insulated glass of the windows meant that this crowd below was completely silent. It made the sight more strange and unnerving. The throng was moving sluggishly down the avenue. There was no sign of police presence, which was odder still.

He got up from the sofa and crossed over to the window.

"Look at this."

She unwrapped herself and came to stand beside him.

"What's going on?"

"I've no idea. It looks like a demonstration."

The scene outside bore an uncanny resemblance to the shreds of meaning he had been able to glean from their one-sided conversation. There was an irony, or a moral hypocrisy to this rambling monologue about inequality, because it came from the mouth of someone who was obviously wealthy. This address would not have been possible otherwise.

He had only known her for five hours, if that could be considered knowing someone. They had met outside her building and she had engaged him in conversation, then she had asked him up. Normally he would have rejected such an offer. Encounters with crazy people happened all the time in the city. But he was naturally introverted and on impulse saw this as an opportunity to break out of his shell. He had thought at first it was about sex but quickly realised that she just wanted to talk. Maybe she was a coke-head.

What she had to say was interesting enough though he didn't completely understand it. Listening to her was like bathing in a poem—a nonsense poem. He let the words cascade around him, pondering one or two and seeing where they led, while she moved on. This resulted in a delay between them that gave him the feeling of being out of phase, further amplified by the silent crowd outside.

"Would you like a sandwich?"

"No thanks."

They had resumed their previous positions. He was already wondering what a chalice was doing on a submarine. Could it be a grail reference? If there was cocaine coursing through her bloodstream, the reference might be more likely drug-related than Arthurian. In which case the chalice was a chillum. Almost a Rastafarian symbol, which itself might be a grail reference.

He could remember a day in London, in Ladbroke Grove. It was a special day. He could not remember why, only that it was significant to Rastafarians. People had heaved their sound systems onto the street. Great stacks of speakers pumped out dub music. Bass frequencies created pressure waves that traversed the body to the bones. Every now and then infinite feedback rang out as King Tubby dialled up the Big Knob.

That day he'd been invited to someone's flat. A friend he had made. A chef. He met his friend's wife for the first time. She had a cloth tied over her head.

"Why do you cover your hair?

"Because Rastafarian women always cover their hair."

"But why?"

It seemed stupid to him. As did Haille Selassie being God. But he was a guest, an outsider invited in, so he kept his mouth shut and listened. A privilege for a white man. There were three other men present, along with his friend and his wife. All earnest and serious, ambitious in their striving for a better world. They seemed like intellectuals, fresh and clean. Music played constantly. Linton Kwesi Johnson—dark and hypnotic, with threatening undertones. The weed was good. He never went back. That was the Chalice.

His attention was drawn again to the window. Something else was going on out there, some kind of violence. There appeared to be a panic. People were moving faster, trying to reach the side streets, climbing over each other. Chaos. But he heard nothing, except his interlocutor, who had wandered from inequality to something more obtuse and John Coltrane who had been softly accompanying them, on and on, over and over. Then he saw three large vehicles coming down the avenue, with ploughs attached. People were fighting back with Molotov cocktails, streaking through the air and bursting into balls of flame.

"And then where would you be? If you discovered that each element was frangible. Not a design. Not something scrawled on cardboard or scratched into wood. It has nothing to do with writing or with any image that can lodge in your mind. No bones in your craw."

The room was beginning to fill with smoke.

"I think the building is on fire."

"What? It's the woman downstairs. She smokes all the time. Where was I? Yes. Halfway out over the lagoon as if tethered by a rope."

The smoke alarms suddenly activated and the sprinklers showered them with water, soaking them to the skin. The apartment was a mess. Status had no meaning at all.

Time to go. But where?

About the Author

Tom Newton is an expatriate English writer. He is the author of *Warfilm* (Bloomsbury 2015) and is the co-founder and co-host of the podcast *The Strange Recital*. After a spell as a seafarer, he has worked for many years in the film industry as a prop man. He has also worked as a musician and sound engineer and was a participant in London's punk music scene in the late 1970s. His areas of interest are art, science, philosophy, music, mythology and meaninglessness. He lives in Woodstock, New York.

A Request

If you enjoyed this book, its publishers and author would be grateful if you would post a short (or long) review on the website where you bought the book and / or on *goodreads.com* or other book review sites. Thanks for reading!

THE STRANGE RECITAL

A PODCAST ABOUT FICTION THAT
QUESTIONS THE NATURE OF REALITY

The Strange Recital is an audio anthology of short fiction.
It is not genre-specific and delights in perceptions of reality
that warp and fold in unexpected ways. The literary works
showcased might be odd, humorous, or surreal. New podcast
episodes are broadcast twice a month. Subscribe at:
www.thestrangerecitalcom

The Strange Recital is also available on: iTunes, Stitcher,
Soundcloud, Google Play Music, Facebook, TuneIn, YouTube,
Spotify, iHeart Radio, and other podcast platforms.

www.thestrangerecital.com

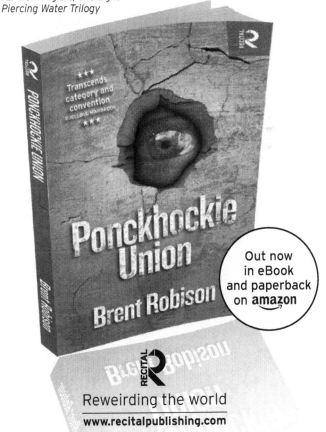

52861455R00112

Made in the USA
Lexington, KY
22 September 2019